INTERNET DETECTIVES

ELECTRONIC MAIL

File   Edit   View   Options   Window   Utilities   Favelist   Help

From: Sent:
To: Subject:

michael coleman
and
allan frewin jones
ACCESS DENIED

OPEN   SEND   FORWARD   REPLY   DELETE   SAVE   PRINT

Mail:

A WORKING PARTNERS BOOK

MACMILLAN CHILDREN'S BOOKS

First published 1997 by Macmillan Children's Books
a division of Macmillan Publishers Limited
25 Eccleston Place, London SW1W 9NF
and Basingstoke

Associated companies throughout the world

Created by Working Partners Limited
London W6 0HE

ISBN 0 330 35113 3

9 8 7 6 5 4 3 2 1

A CIP catalogue record for this book is available from
the British Library.

Printed and bound in Great Britain by Mackays of Chatham plc, Kent

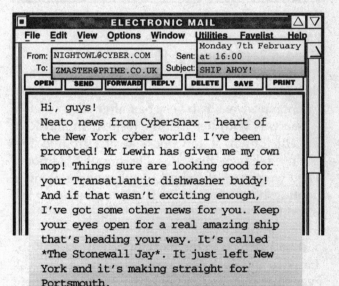

CHAPTER 1

■ **ELECTRONIC MAIL** △ ▽

File   Edit   View   Options   Window   Utilities   Favelist   Help

From: NIGHTOWL@CYBER.COM   Sent: Monday 7th February at 16:00

To: ZMASTER@PRIME.CO.UK   Subject: SHIP AHOY!

| OPEN | SEND | FORWARD | REPLY | DELETE | SAVE | PRINT |

Hi, guys!
Neato news from CyberSnax – heart of
the New York cyber world! I've been
promoted! Mr Lewin has given me my own
mop! Things sure are looking good for
your Transatlantic dishwasher buddy!
And if that wasn't exciting enough,
I've got some other news for you. Keep
your eyes open for a real amazing ship
that's heading your way. It's called
The Stonewall Jay. It just left New
York and it's making straight for
Portsmouth.
Check it out, guys! It's an ex-US Navy
warship. It was bought by some big
company and fixed up so it looks
exactly the way it did during World
War Two. They do guided tours of
the engine-room and the bridge and

everything. Even the new luxury cruise cabins!

I went aboard while it was in New York, and it was a gas.

Heck! My new mop is hollering at me to go swab some floors. Catch you soon, guys.

Mitch 'Aharr! Jim, lad,' Zanelli

Mail:

Portsmouth, England.
Monday 21st February, 10 a.m.

It was one of those bright, sunlit February days that made Tamsyn Smith feel that maybe winter in England wasn't so very bad after all.

She was with her friends, Josh Allan and Rob Zanelli, down at the docks which fronted the enclosed haven that was Portsmouth Harbour. They were part of a short queue moving along a floating boom towards a large, impressive grey warship.

The Stonewall Jay.

It had arrived in the harbour on Saturday. Rob, Tamsyn and Josh had been awaiting its arrival ever since they had received the e-mail from their American friend, Mitch.

Although Mitch and Rob shared the same last name, they weren't related so far as they knew. Rob had contacted Mitch some time ago via the Internet, and they had become firm, if separated, friends.

As this was half-term week, Rob and the others had decided to avoid the rush of eager beavers over the weekend and leave their visit until the initial scrum had subsided a little.

Behind them, in permanent dry dock, the familiar dark shape of HMS Victory lifted its spiky masts and web-like rigging into the brilliant blue sky.

Rob looked at the drab grey shape of the Stonewall Jay and then ran his eyes over the romantic contours of the old eighteenth-century warship.

He pointed to the Victory. 'Now that,' he said, 'is what I call a proper warship. Launched in 1765. 104 guns. Crew of 850 officers and men. And on the 21st of October, 1805, Admiral Lord Nelson was fatally wounded whilst leading the British fleet to victory against—'

'Oh, stop showing off, Rob,' Tamsyn said with a laugh. 'Anyone in the world could get information like that off the Internet.'

'True,' admitted Rob, 'but they'd have to *remember* it as well. That's the difference.'

Josh got behind Rob's wheelchair to assist Tamsyn in pushing their friend up the slope. Rob had lost the use of his legs in a car crash five years ago when he had been eight years old.

The Stonewall Jay had limited wheelchair access, which meant Rob could take a good look around above decks; but there was no way he could join his friends for the full guided tour.

'Don't worry about it,' he said as they came

onto the deck. 'There's plenty to look at up here. And *you* can tell me about all the other stuff.'

The small group of visitors was gathered together by a ramrod-stiff man in a crisp, smart US Navy Uniform.

'Welcome aboard the US Stonewall Jay,' the man said in a strong Australian accent. 'I hope you have an interesting, enjoyable and informative tour, and I would remind you that visitors are asked to keep to the main designated tour routes at all times, as signified by the yellow arrows.'

'Excuse me,' Tamsyn said to the man as they manoeuvred Rob's wheelchair out of the main huddle of people. 'I've been wondering about this ever since I found out the ship's name. What kind of a bird is a Stonewall Jay? I've looked the name up all over the place, but I can't find it anywhere.'

The crewman smiled. 'It isn't named after a bird, miss. Stonewall Jay is short for Stonewall Jackson. He was a general in the American Civil War.'

'Oh, I see.' Well, that was one mystery solved.

There were about twenty people in the group to which Tamsyn and Josh attached themselves. They gave Rob a wave as they headed in through a small, narrow entrance.

Rob turned and made his way down to the stern where two massive gun turrets squatted threateningly on the deck, pointing their once deadly weapons away towards Portsdown Hill.

Josh and Tamsyn trooped along with the rest as

the tour led them along narrow corridors and up steep, cramped stairways towards the bridge.

They crammed together in the wheelhouse.

'This ship,' announced their guide, 'was built in 1923. It is 160 metres long and has a beam, at the widest point, of 25 metres. It held a crew of 727 officers and men, and could steam at a maximum of 21 knots. If you take a look through the window, here, you will see the forward gun turret, consisting of an armoured barbette, and two twelve-inch guns.'

Josh peered through the lofty window down at the bow of the ship. 'Twelve inches?' he said to Tamsyn. 'That's about 30 centimetres, isn't it? What a titchy little gun for such a big ship.'

'That's not how *long* they were, twit! I think he means the bullets it shot were twelve inches *across*,' Tamsyn said, over the continuing voice of their guide.

'I know. I was kidding. And you mean *shells*,' Josh corrected her. 'Big guns like that fire *shells*, not bullets.'

'Thanks, Josh,' said Tamsyn, giving him a look. 'I'm glad you told me that. Look, I'm not inter-ested in how they went around blowing things up. I want to know what things were like for the crew and stuff like that.'

As the snake of tourists made its way down below decks, their guide poured out a continuous stream of information. A steep descent took them to the engine room. The ship's engines were massive.

'Wow,' said Josh, gazing at the huge machinery. 'Amazing! We could do with one of these in our washing machine – it's always breaking down.'

'Keep up, Josh,' Tamsyn threw back as the tour moved on. 'You don't want to get lost.'

The guide led them out of the engine room. The sudden change from the drab grey walls and functional appearance of the rest of the ship was quite dramatic. There were carpets in this area, and brass light fittings and pristine paintwork, as well as the smell of polish and air freshener.

'This area was originally the crew's quarters,' he told them. 'But now they've been converted into berths for travellers who want to experience a cruise with a difference.'

The tour did an about-turn and set off towards the boiler room. They came into the room on an upper gallery.

Tamsyn stared down into the great dark gulf. Her imagination peopled the room with sweating stokers, shovelling coal into the huge greedy boilers while the ship ploughed through the water into battle.

'It reminds me of that old black and white film,' Tamsyn said. 'You know? The one all about that ship in the Second World War.' She looked round to Josh. 'Know the one I mean?'

A strange face stared at her.

'Oh, sorry. I thought you were … er …' She peered over the woman's shoulder, expecting to see Josh's cheerful face and tousled hair some-where back there.

Her brows knitted. Where was Josh? It wasn't as if he was particularly *unobtrusive*. Josh was the sort of person you noticed in a crowd.

'If you'd all follow me,' called the guide, 'we'll be observing the shell hoist and the port gun turret next.'

Where the heck has Josh got to? People pushed past Tamsyn as she looked around for a sign of him.

The guide's voice faded out of Tamsyn's earshot as she hung back, hoping to see Josh come hurrying along to catch them up.

Josh didn't appear.

'Oh, brilliant, Josh,' Tamsyn grumbled to herself. 'Trust you!'

She took a final irritated glance over her shoulder towards where they were *meant* to have gone. Then she headed back the way they had come.

I suppose I'd better go and find him, before he gets himself into trouble, Tamsyn thought.

Then she heard it!

A wild, frantic, high-pitched screaming which echoed along the narrow corridor.

Her heart in her mouth, Tamsyn ran towards the horrible noise. It sounded like a *murder* was going on back there!

CHAPTER 2

Tamsyn ran into the luxury cruise area of the ship. The screeching noise was louder now, as she ran helter-skelter down a plush corridor and around the bend of an abrupt T-junction.

It was clear to her that the frantic noise wasn't coming from a human throat. It was an animal. An animal in distress.

She ran a few faltering steps, turning her head to try and pinpoint the exact direction from which the noise originated. It was coming from behind a cabin door a little way further up the narrow corridor. Now that she was closer, she could hear that it was mixed in with thumps and the harsh voice of a man shouting.

Tamsyn darted forwards. On the door was the number 15. She yanked the door handle down and pushed. The door sprang open, but before Tamsyn had a moment to orientate herself, something came hurtling through the air straight at her face.

She instinctively raised her arms to protect herself. She saw teeth and claws and wild eyes, and her ears were filled with shrill screams.

Her eyes shut automatically as a heavy weight thudded against her forearms, sending her reeling backwards.

A man's voice shouted.

In an instant the creature had bounced away from her, its cries echoing around the enclosed space.

Shocked and alarmed, Tamsyn dropped her arms and stared into the cabin.

She saw a narrow unmade bed and a table under a curtained porthole. On the table was a crate with one opened side. There were stencilled markings on the side and a scattering of what looked like straw and pieces of fruit on the floor of the crate and on the carpet beneath the table.

Tamsyn only had a moment or two to take this in before a man loomed into sight. He was short and stocky, with slicked-back, greasy, black hair and a thin moustache. He had red claw-marks down one flabby cheek, and his expression was cruel and angry.

Tamsyn locked eyes with him for a split second before he slammed the door in her face.

'Hey!' yelled Tamsyn, beating on the door with the heels of both hands. 'What's going on in there?'

She tried the handle again, but the door didn't budge. The man must have locked it from inside.

She hauled uselessly at the handle as a flurry of noise erupted again. There were banging and crashing sounds, as though the man was stumbling around the cabin trying to catch the animal.

The screeching reached a crescendo and a few moments later became muffled.

Tamsyn heard the crash of a hammer on wood and then a sudden, startling quiet.

Tamsyn hit the door again. 'Let me in! What are you *doing* to that animal?' She was afraid that the man had killed it to shut it up.

Then she heard a thin, high-pitched whimpering accompanied by a frantic scrabbling of claws.

The animal was alive.

Tamsyn shot a look in both directions along the corridor. It was unbelievable that no one else had come to check out the cause of all the uproar. The only explanation had to be that everyone had quit this part of the ship when it had docked. Everyone, that is, except the man in the cabin.

'I'm going to get someone!' Tamsyn shouted through the closed door. 'Just you wait!'

She had no time to stop and think. All Tamsyn knew was that there was an animal in distress, and that something had to be done about it.

She ran back the way she had come.

There were voices up ahead.

'I wasn't doing anything wrong! I just lost track of the others, that's all. You don't have to treat me like I was some kind of criminal.'

It was Josh. Tamsyn rounded a corner.

Josh was standing between two uniformed crewmen.

'Don't you have ears, boy?' said one of the men. 'Didn't you hear when you were told to keep with the guide?'

'Yes, but … Oh! Tamsyn, hi! These two—'

Tamsyn came to a skidding halt.

'Back there!' she panted. 'There's a man … in a cabin … with an animal. I think it's hurt or something. You've got to—'

'Another kid!' said the first crewman. 'What do you think this ship is? An adventure playground? Everyone was told up front not to go wandering off.'

'I didn't wander off,' Josh explained. 'I got lost.'

'You've got to do something!' Tamsyn yelled in exasperation. 'I'm sure that animal was being mistreated.'

'There are no animals on this ship,' said the second man.

'Oh, really?' Tamsyn said. She glared at him. 'I saw it! I nearly got knocked flying by it. It's back there, and if you're not prepared to do anything about it, then I'm going to find someone who will.'

'Whoa, there,' said the first man. 'You're not going anywhere. The pair of you are leaving this ship right now.'

'This is ridiculous,' said Tamsyn. 'I want to speak to the captain. That animal back there is—'

'There are no animals on this ship,' said the second crewman again. He seemed absolutely determined not to believe Tamsyn.

A hand came down on her shoulder and the two friends were marched along in tandem.

Tamsyn was fuming. 'I'm going to call the

RSPCA the moment I get off,' she said. 'Even if you don't believe me, they will.'

'Sure,' said the first man in an annoyingly patronizing way. 'You just do that little thing.'

Rob had done a complete circle of the deck. The Stonewall Jay had some fascinating things about it, but he decided he still preferred the eighteenth-century splendour of the HMS Victory.

He glanced down over the bow and was surprised to see the small figures of Tamsyn and Josh, marching rapidly towards the building which housed the booking office for the tour.

Well, Tamsyn was marching. Josh was trotting along in her wake. Even at such a distance, Rob recognized the determined set of Tamsyn's shoulders. Something had clearly upset her. He glanced at his watch. According to the leaflet, the tour should still be in full swing. So why had his two companions left the ship?

By the time he reached the swing doors that led into the office, Tamsyn and Josh were coming out.

'What's up?' he asked. 'Did you get seasick?'

'Tamsyn saw an animal on the ship,' Josh explained. 'She thought it was being mistreated.'

Rob looked at Tamsyn. 'An animal?' he said. 'Are you sure?'

'Don't you start!' Tamsyn said angrily. She waved an arm behind her. 'That's exactly what they said. Of course I'm sure. The poor thing was screaming its head off.'

'Sorry,' Rob said, lifting his hands in a placatory way. 'What sort of animal was it?'

Tamsyn frowned. 'A monkey kind of thing,' she said. 'It had golden brown fur, and lots of fur all around its face. You should have seen the little crate it was being kept in. The monkey was about this big.' She held her hands about 35 centimetres apart; then she spread them to about 70 centimetres. 'And the crate was only about this square. It can't be legal to keep an animal cooped up like that.'

'Tamsyn wanted to phone the RSPCA from in there,' Josh said, hooking his head towards the booking office. 'But they wouldn't let her.'

'You can phone from my house,' Rob said.

'Good,' said Tamsyn. 'I'll do that. Let's go right now. And I hope that rotten, slimy pig gets prosecuted and put in jail.'

Josh and Rob looked at one another. When Tamsyn got mad, she really got mad!

Manor House, Portsmouth. 4 p.m.
Rob and Josh looked on while Tamsyn finished her phone call.

'Yes,' she said into the receiver. 'I understand. Thanks for trying, anyway.'

She put the receiver down and slumped into an armchair in the Zanellis' living room.

It had been a frustrating few hours for Tamsyn. She had been on the phone to the RSPCA within a minute of arriving at Rob's house. She had explained clearly and precisely what she had seen, and the person at the other end of the phone had said they would investigate.

She had phoned them hourly ever since, but there had been no news until now. And the news was *not* what Tamsyn had been hoping to hear.

'So?' Josh asked. 'What's happened?'

'They sent a couple of officers over there,' Tamsyn said glumly, 'but they didn't find anything. None of the crew admitted knowing anything about a monkey being on board, and there was no trace of an animal anywhere in the cabin.'

'I suppose that bloke you saw must have packed it up in its crate and hidden it somewhere,' Josh said.

'Or maybe he brought it ashore?' Rob suggested.

'He can't have done that,' Tamsyn said. 'What about the quarantine laws? You can't just bring animals into this country without going through quarantine.'

'You shouldn't, you mean,' Rob said.

'Perhaps it was a pet,' Josh said. 'People some-times keep pretty inappropriate animals as pets.'

'If it was, then it was the angriest pet I've ever seen,' said Tamsyn. She shook her head. 'Even if a person did have a pet monkey, they wouldn't keep it in a horrible little wooden box like that. And surely other people on the ship would know about it?'

'Whatever it was,' Rob said with a shrug, 'we've done everything we can about it.'

Tamsyn looked at him. 'I don't think so,' she said with quiet determination.

'If you're cooking up plans for boarding that ship at the dead of night like some kind of secret agent, you can think again,' Josh said. 'For a start, that man could have hidden the monkey any-where. And for a finish – we'll get caught.'

'And probably court-martialled and keel-hauled,' added Rob.

'What's keelhauled, when it's at home?' asked Josh.

'You get tied to a rope and dragged right under the ship.'

'Nasty!' Josh said.

'If you two have quite finished making a big joke out of this!' Tamsyn said angrily. 'I don't think there's anything particularly funny about cruelty to animals.'

'Calm down, Tamsyn,' Rob said. 'Neither do we. Look, you've phoned the RSPCA. What else can you do?'

'We can find out exactly what sort of monkey it was, to be getting on with,' Tamsyn said. 'And we can try and find out if the numbers and letters on that crate mean anything. That way we might be able to work out where it came from.'

'Can you remember them?' Rob asked.

Tamsyn screwed her eyes tight shut. 'I think so,' she said, trying to form a mental image of the slice of the cabin that she had seen for a moment before the man had slammed the door on her. 'It started off with a U and then an S. Yes, that's right. Then it went: N, S, S, 2050. Then there was an oblique followed by … um … 773. No, wait, 733. That was it. USNSS, 2050 stroke 733.'

'Blimey,' Josh said with a whistle. 'Well remembered!'

'I've got an idea,' Rob said. 'Six heads are better than three, aren't they? Why don't we e-mail the others? We can give them a description of the monkey and let them get to work on the markings on the crate at the same time.'

By the others, Rob meant their overseas Internet friends. They had already solved several mysteries together in the past. Mitch Zanelli lived in New York, Lauren King in Canada and Tom Peterson in Australia.

'Great idea,' Josh said. 'Mitch should be able to work out what the markings are. I mean, he's American, after all – and so is the ship.'

'It was, you mean,' Rob said. 'According to their leaflet, it belongs to an Australian corporation now. They're the ones who did all the work and turned it into a cruising museum-ship.'

'Let's not just sit here chatting,' Tamsyn said. 'Let's get to work.' She looked over her shoulder at her friends as she headed for the door.

'I'll tell you one thing for certain,' she said as they followed her along the hall to Rob's ground floor bedroom, where his computer was set up. 'No way was that monkey a pet.' Her eyes narrowed. 'There's something cruel and horrible going on in that ship, and I'm going to find out what, if it's the last thing I do.'

CHAPTER 3

Manor House. 21st February, 4.15 p.m.

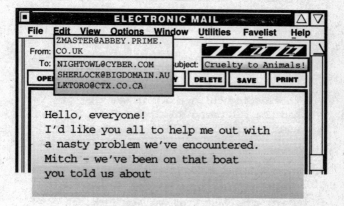

```
┌─────────────────────────────────────────────────────┐
│ ■           ELECTRONIC MAIL              △ ▽          │
│ File  Edit  View  Options  Window  Utilities  Favelist  Help │
│        ZMASTER@ABBEY.PRIME.                           │
│ From:  CO.UK                                          │
│ To:  NIGHTOWL@CYBER.COM      ubject: Cruelty to Animals! │
│      SHERLOCK@BIGDOMAIN.AU                             │
│ OPE  LKTORO@CTX.CO.CA     Y   DELETE  SAVE   PRINT     │
│                                                       │
│   Hello, everyone!                                    │
│   I'd like you all to help me out with                │
│   a nasty problem we've encountered.                  │
│   Mitch - we've been on that boat                     │
│   you told us about                                   │
└─────────────────────────────────────────────────────┘
```

'Ship,' Rob said.
'Sorry?' Tamsyn paused at the keyboard.
'It's a ship, not a boat.'
'Oh, honestly!'

```
Mitch - we've been on that ship you
told us about. There was an animal on
board and it looked to me as if it was
being very badly treated. We tried to
```

do something for it, but the man who was with it must have hidden it. We're investigating *three* things.
Lauren - that new animals CD-ROM you told us about should help with the first thing.

1. The animal. It's a sort of monkey, about 35-40 centimetres tall and has a long tail. It has long fingers with long claws. I remember long golden brown fur, including a lot of thick fur all around its face. It screeches when it's unhappy and it has plenty of teeth!

2. The crate. There was a crate in the cabin where I saw the animal. The interesting thing about it was that it had the following markings on it: USNSS2050/733. Any ideas, people?

3. The ship. I don't think the monkey was a pet owned by a crew member. So, a passenger must have brought it on board. The last stop was New York. Mitch - any ideas? Do you know where the ship had been previously?

I'm determined to help that animal if I can, so get back to us with any info you can find.
Thanks.

Tamsyn

Mail:

Tamsyn re-read the message, then clicked SEND to dispatch her request instantaneously around the world to their three friends.

'OK,' she said, 'that's got the others on the case. Now let's see what *we* can come up with.'

Perth, Australia.
Tuesday 22nd February, 8 a.m.

Tom Peterson was sitting with his parents in their sunlit kitchen, eating breakfast and making some last-second alterations to his homework.

'You should have done that last night, Tom,' Mrs Peterson grumbled as she put a plate in front of him. 'I ought to ban you from playing with that computer until all your school work is out of the way.'

Tom smiled up at her. 'But it helps with my school work, Mum,' he said. 'Don't you remember what Mr Lillee said at the last parents' evening? He said—'

'Computers are the educational tools of the future,' interrupted Tom's mother. 'Yes, I know. But you were playing games on it all yesterday evening. You tell me what's educational about that, eh?'

Tom flexed his fingers. 'It sharpens up your reflexes,' he said with a grin. 'And it keeps your brain alert, doesn't it, Dad?'

His father looked up from some documents he was reading. 'Huh?'

'I was just explaining to Mum,' Tom said, 'using computers keeps your brain active.'

'Don't talk to me about computers right now,' Mr Peterson growled. 'We've been on the trail of a hacker for the past six months. He even had the cheek to hack into the police computer! We'd almost nailed the blighter when he stopped. We haven't heard a peep out of him for three weeks now.'

'A hacker?' Tom said with a whistle. 'What did he do: hack into bank files and steal loads of money?'

'No.' Mr Peterson shoved the papers into his briefcase and closed it. 'Filefly isn't that sort of hacker. He just likes to cause mayhem. And he did, too. Plenty of it! And then, just when we were closing in on him, he stopped. But we'll nail him. No one hacks into a police computer and gets away with it!'

'I've heard about hackers,' said Mrs Peterson. 'They break into private computer files, don't they? But if this Filefly fellow wasn't out to steal anything, what's the point?'

'The *point* is to cause the maximum disruption,' said Mr Peterson as he got up. 'Hackers like Filefly get a big kick out of causing a whole heap of chaos. These days, most companies rely almost entirely on their computers. It only takes one idiot hacker getting into their system, to screw up the works for days on end. Millions of dollars are lost every year because of hackers like Filefly.'

'And you reckon Filefly's gone to ground, huh, Dad?' asked Tom.

Mr Peterson nodded. 'He'll turn up again. These people always do. It's like they can't help themselves.' He tucked his briefcase under his arm and headed for the door. 'And when he does – chkkk!' He made a cutting gesture across his throat. 'We'll nab him!'

Tom chewed his breakfast thoughtfully after his father had left for work. Hackers weren't dumb. Maybe Filefly had realized the police were hot on his trail.

'Where are you going?' asked Mrs Peterson suspiciously as Tom slid quietly out of the kitchen.

'Nowhere,' Tom called back.

'Nowhere, my foot!' called his mother. 'You're off to play with that computer again!'

'Only for a couple of minutes,' Tom called. 'I've got plenty of time before I have to leave for school.'

He booted up the computer and waited the few seconds it took for his files to come online. Maybe there was a way in which Filefly could be flushed out. From the little he did know about hackers, Tom knew they couldn't resist bragging about what they were up to. Hackers couldn't help themselves. The obvious way forward was for Tom to make some discreet enquiries through the local Internet scene.

```
MAIL: 1 MESSAGE WAITING
```

Tom opened his mail and quickly read Tamsyn's message.

'Sorry, guys,' he murmured as he cleared the screen, 'I'll have to take a rain check on that. I've got other fish to fry right now! I've got a big, bad, bold hacker to hunt down.'

Tom grinned to himself as he began to write a tempting message for the local Net bulletin board.

```
I am looking for a partner to help me with
some fun computer work. Preferably someone
who knows how to find *files*, someone with
their own *axe* to grind and someone who likes
to use the Net to *fly*. Satisfaction and
complete confidentiality guaranteed. No
wimps, nerds or time-wasters, please!
```

He leaned back and folded his arms. Now all he had to do was wait for a reply. If Filefly was out there, that message should reel him in like a fish on a line!

'Tom! School!' Tom was brought abruptly out of his blissful daydream by his mother's commanding voice.

He closed the computer down and left the room. He could hardly wait for the school day to end so he could get back and see what might be waiting for him that afternoon.

Josh's house, Portsmouth. 3 p.m.

Josh was sprawled across the couch like a discarded rag doll. He'd brought down a heap of old computer magazines from his bedroom and was happily re-reading them. He had one eye on the TV, where one lot of weird-looking cartoon characters were busy blasting another bunch of mutant blob-things off the screen.

The doorbell rang.

Rats! thought Josh, alone in the house. *No sooner do I get myself comfortable than some twerp has to ring the doorbell.* He reluctantly heaved himself up off the couch and mooched out into the hall.

He pulled the door open.

'Hello, Josh!' The boy who stood there was Josh's age. He was smaller and skinnier than Josh, with a narrow, pale, freckly face and a ginger crew-cut.

'Ritchie?' Josh blurted in astonishment. 'What on earth are you doing here?'

The ginger-haired boy laughed.

'Let me in and I'll tell you,' he said.

Josh opened the door fully and Ritchie stepped over the threshold as if he turned up on the doorstep every day.

But the fact was that Josh hadn't seen his old primary school friend Ritchie Moore for three years!

CHAPTER 4

Josh was delighted to see his old friend again so unexpectedly. He grabbed a couple of Coke cans out of the fridge, and the two boys headed up to his bedroom.

'You're supposed to be in Australia,' Josh said. 'What happened?'

Ritchie grinned at him. 'We came back,' he said. 'My mum couldn't stand it down there.'

Josh opened his bedroom door and they went inside.

'Which bit couldn't she stand?' Josh asked. 'The brilliant weather? The beaches? The open spaces? The clean air?'

'The insects,' Ritchie said. 'The lizards and spiders and creepy-crawlies and mozzies.' He stared around Josh's untidy room with its wall-to-wall scattering of computer magazines and other debris.

'Ah,' Josh said, nodding. 'Yeah, I can see that. No problem.' Josh wasn't a big fan of things with more than four legs – especially those which lurked in dark corners and scuttled out at you unexpectedly.

Ritchie's family had emigrated to Australia three years ago. Ritchie had been one of Josh's best friends at primary school, and his departure down under had been quite a wrench for both of them. They had promised to keep in touch, but after a brief flurry of letters (which got shorter and shorter), they lost contact. The last time Josh had written to Ritchie had been two years ago, when he sent a birthday card. There hadn't been a reply.

'Where is it, then?' asked Ritchie.

Josh looked at him. 'Where's what?'

'The computer. You must have a computer. I thought everyone had their own computer these days.' Ritchie looked at Josh with pale blue eyes. 'Haven't you got one? I have.'

Then Josh remembered something else about Ritchie. Even as a small boy, he had always liked to go one better than everyone else.

'There didn't seem much point in buying one for home,' Josh said. 'I can use the computers at school. And I can use my mate Rob's whenever I like.'

Ritchie's lip curled. 'It's not the same,' he said. 'I'd be bored stupid in the evenings if I didn't have my own computer to use whenever I felt like it.' He gave Josh a grin. 'You'll have to come over and try mine out.'

'Yeah, I'd like to,' Josh said. 'Meanwhile, you can tell me all about Australia. Hey, I just thought! You lived in Freemantle, didn't you?'

'That's right. Why?'

'I've got a really good pal on the Internet who lives in Perth,' said Josh. 'That's just up the coast from Freemantle, isn't it? You might have come across him on the Net. Tom Peterson?'

Ritchie shook his head. 'I don't think so,' he said. 'I didn't spend much time gabbing to other people – except for one or two *special blokes* I knew.'

Josh gave him a quizzical look.

Ritchie grinned at him. 'Blokes who know how to use computers to have fun,' he said. 'Know what I mean?'

Josh wasn't entirely sure he did, but before he had the chance to say so, Ritchie had embarked on a long description of the computer he had at home and all the state-of-the-art software he possessed.

At primary school, the two boys had been as keen as each other on computers, but judging by the way Ritchie was speaking now, his keenness had turned into a full-blown obsession.

In fact, Ritchie didn't seem in the least bit interested in anything else. But neither did he seem to know much about the latest games, or chatlines, or any of the usual Internet services.

And Josh found that a bit odd.

Toronto, Canada. 5.45 p.m.

'Allie? Do you want anything to eat?' Lauren King called out. She was in the kitchen of the small third floor apartment where she lived with her grandmother and was fixing herself some waffles and syrup.

'Not right now, thanks, dear,' Allie called back. The grey-haired old lady was busy at the computer that sat in the corner of their lounge. She was playing Hangman, and she was about to lose.

She frowned as the screen flashed up:

BAD LUCK. WANT TO TRY AGAIN?

Allie clicked NO and set off in search of other interesting web sites. Lauren came into the lounge and perched on the chair next to her.

'I've finished my homework,' Lauren said. 'Can I take a look through Animals Unlimited now?'

'Of course you can,' said Allie.

Lauren had been dying to get to the computer and use her new CD-ROM ever since she'd got home from school that afternoon to find Tamsyn's call for help waiting. Allie had one very strict rule: homework came first, no matter how important incoming e-mails might seem.

Lauren was twelve. She had lived with her gran ever since her parents had died. Between them, Lauren and Allie would have kept their computer busy right round the clock if there weren't other things they had to do.

Lauren had known her Internet friends for some time now, although she was still careful to keep her age secret. That was one of the great things about the Internet – you could make friends with people of all ages. After all, Mitch, down in New York, was seventeen, and yet he treated her as an equal.

Allie shifted over to give Lauren access to the computer. Lauren pressed the button and the CD tray shot out. She carefully placed the CD-ROM disk in position and shut the tray again.

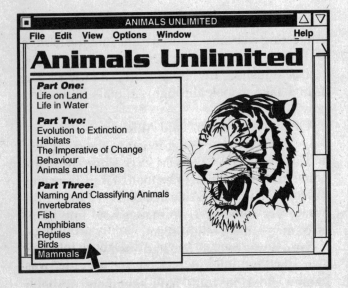

Lauren clicked on the *Mammals* button and a second menu appeared.

File   Edit   View   Options   Window   Help

Animals Unlimited

Sub-Class Prototheria
Sub-Class Theria
Order Marsupalia
Order Monotremata
     Infra-Class Metatheria
     Infra-Class Eutheria
Order Primates

'That's the one we want,' Allie said, pointing to
Order Primates. 'If Tamsyn's animal is a monkey,
it'll be in there.'

'Well, I sure hope so,' Lauren said, gazing at the
tongue-twisting list of *Orders* and *Sub-Classes* and
Infra-Classes.

Clicking on *Order Primates* brought Lauren to
yet another menu. This time of Family groupings.

Now things started to get much more interesting. Every animal described in the file was
pictured alongside plenty of data about its habi-
tat, lifestyle and bullet point facts about size and
breeding. Lauren worked her way slowly through
a whole menagerie of primates. Fortunately, the
full-colour pictures of the animals being
described made it easy for Lauren to discard at a

glance tree-shrews, aye-ayes, loris, pottos, bush-babies and tarsiers.

SUB-ORDER ANTHROPOIDEA

This sub-order includes the higher primates and is divided into two infra-orders.

FAMILY CALLITRICHIDAE

Marmosets and tamarins: 21 Species.

'Hey, Allie,' Lauren murmured as she worked her way through the file. 'This looks more like it.'

She halted the file scrolling up the screen.

'Bingo!' she said. 'Got it!'

ANIMALS UNLIMITED

File   Edit   View   Options   Window   Help

Animals Unlimited

GOLDEN LION TAMARIN

The golden lion tamarin is one of the most endangered of all mammals. It lives in a tiny part of the Brazilian forest. It spends all its life in the forest canopy. If threatened it can be extremely aggressive - baring its teeth, expanding its mane and giving out high-pitched shrieks.

Since 1960, it has been illegal to capture or export this animal, although this has not stopped poachers from trading in golden lion tamarins, despite the fact that it is on the brink of extinction.

Lauren read the file with a growing sense of disquiet.

'Well, if Tamsyn's monkey really is a golden lion tamarin,' she said to her gran, 'then the sooner she gets to take a look at this file, the better.'

CHAPTER 5

Manor House, Portsmouth.
Wednesday 23rd February, 11.30 a.m.

Rob sat at his computer with a frustrated frown furrowing his brow. Josh was leaning over his shoulder, similarly baffled.

The screen showed the Net Navigator menu page. They had returned to it after fruitless attempts at trying to discover what the markings that Tamsyn had seen on the crate could possibly mean.

They hadn't even come close to finding the answer. They had explored the *Travel* section, hoping to find a World Wide Web site set up by the owners of the Stonewall Jay. They found nothing.

They pored through *Entertainment*. Maybe the museum ship was cross-referenced in there somewhere? The result was the same. They found holiday sites and cruise sites in *Travel*, and they found floating restaurants under *Entertainment*. But nothing to throw even a glimmer of light onto what USNSS2050/733 might mean.

Lauren's e-mail identifying the animal as a golden lion tamarin had been waiting for Rob that morning. At least that would be something positive to show Tamsyn when she arrived. Meanwhile, the two boys were determined not to be defeated by the markings.

'Maybe your mate, Ritchie, might be able to come up with some ideas for where to look?' Rob said as he idly slid the cursor from section to section without bothering to click. 'I'm blowed if I can think of anything else.'

Josh nodded. 'I'll ask him,' he said. 'But only as a last resort. He can be a bit big-headed, to be honest, and I don't want him to think we don't know what we're doing.'

Rob glanced around at him. 'I thought you said you were mates?'

Josh nodded. 'We were. That doesn't mean I think he's *perfect*. I can be mates with people who are a bit peculiar,' he grinned. 'I mean, we're mates, aren't we?'

Rob looked at him. 'What's that supposed to mean?' he said with a laugh. 'Are you suggesting I'm peculiar?'

Josh screwed his face up. 'Well, no more than Tamsyn, I don't suppose.'

'Oh thanks!'

Josh frowned at the screen. 'Maybe we're going at this in the wrong way?' he said. 'I mean, we've been trying to work out what the marks mean by looking for something about the Stonewall Jay itself. Maybe that's not the best way of going about it?'

'OK,' Rob said. 'Let's do a keyword search, and see if that takes us anywhere.'

'Just type in the letters first,' Josh suggested.

Rob typed in USNSS and clicked for a response.

```
Search results.
Found 10 matches for USNSS.
```

'Way to go!' Josh said. 'Let's check them out. Get 'em all up on screen, Rob. We're on our way!'

The ten matches were revealed.

'On our way to nowhere,' Rob sighed. Most were concerned with seismic activity – earthquakes! And the rest were well wide of the mark.

'And for our next bright idea,' Rob said drily. He looked around at Josh. 'Well?'

'Beats me.'

'Wait a minute!' Rob clicked his fingers. 'Let's try an acronym search.'

The search engine found 36,263 documents about ACRONYMS.

'I'll go and get my sleeping bag, shall I?' said Josh. 'It looks like we're going to be here a while.'

'Don't panic,' said Rob. 'They'll be divided up into sections.' He clicked and the screen changed. 'There you go!'

Glossary of Acronyms

Rob's fingers pecked at the keyboard and a few moments later a new list appeared on screen.

Ugly Socialites Need Sympathy Society

Umpires Society of North Saskatchewan (Seniors)

United Society of Newts, Salamanders and Snakes

United Southern News: Syndicated Section

United States Naval Supply System

Urban Slackers News: Sub-pop Seattle

Usual Suspects: Never Say Surrender

Uxorious Spouses Network: Stay Single

'There's our baby!' Rob said, sliding the cursor up to *United States Naval Supply System*.

'Of course!' Josh said. 'The Stonewall Jay was part of the US Navy originally.'

'And when they sold the ship, they threw in all the fixtures and fittings,' Rob said. 'Including that crate. Rats! The markings aren't going to give us any clues about the tamarin at all.'

'Mabye not,' Josh countered. 'But it wouldn't hurt to check it out. Can you get into that site?'

Rob tried to access the site.

Rob looked round at his friend. 'Well, that's not very welcoming,' he said. 'There's no way of getting in there, so that's as far as we can go with the markings on the crate.'

'Oh well,' said Josh, 'at least Lauren's come up with some useful stuff. I wonder how Tom and Mitch are doing?'

New York, USA. 7.30 a.m.

The CyberSnax café off Central Park was empty and strangely quiet in the early New York morning. Mr Lewin was checking stock and Mitch was indulging in a pre-opening time session on one of the café's Net-linked computers. A cup of cappuccino steamed at his elbow as he guided the cursor across the screen.

There you go, he murmured to himself, *I thought you'd be in here, somewhere.*

Mitch was always willing to help his British Net friends, and he was as concerned about the welfare of the animal Tamsyn had seen as all the others.

Mitch had remembered reading an article about the Stonewall Jay in the *New York Times* a few weeks back: it had prompted him to visit the ship. Once he knew what he was looking for, it didn't take him long to log into the archives site of the newspaper and home in on the article in question.

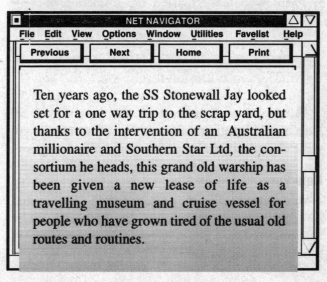

Ten years ago, the SS Stonewall Jay looked set for a one way trip to the scrap yard, but thanks to the intervention of an Australian millionaire and Southern Star Ltd, the consortium he heads, this grand old warship has been given a new lease of life as a travelling museum and cruise vessel for people who have grown tired of the usual old routes and routines.

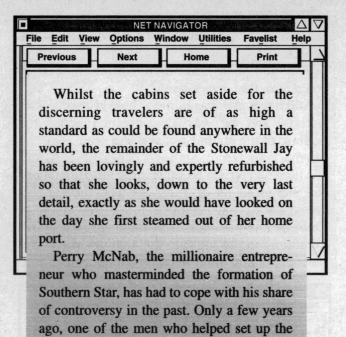

Whilst the cabins set aside for the discerning travelers are of as high a standard as could be found anywhere in the world, the remainder of the Stonewall Jay has been lovingly and expertly refurbished so that she looks, down to the very last detail, exactly as she would have looked on the day she first steamed out of her home port.

Perry McNab, the millionaire entrepreneur who masterminded the formation of Southern Star, has had to cope with his share of controversy in the past. Only a few years ago, one of the men who helped set up the

Mitch skipped the rest. It was just a load of *blah* about Southern Star Ltd and some illegal stuff that one of the directors of the company had got up to some years previously. Nothing relevant, from what he could make out at a quick glance. But as he scrolled the file down, he came across the thing he had especially remembered.

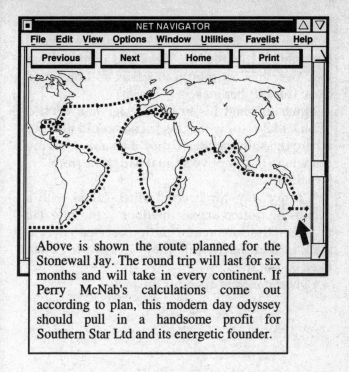

Above is shown the route planned for the Stonewall Jay. The round trip will last for six months and will take in every continent. If Perry McNab's calculations come out according to plan, this modern day odyssey should pull in a handsome profit for Southern Star Ltd and its energetic founder.

'Hey, Brainiac!' Mr Lewin's voice hollered out from the back room, breaking into Mitch's concentration. 'Are we gonna open up today, or are we taking a vacation I don't know about?'

'I'm on my way,' Mitch called as he rapidly cleared the screen and clicked for the e-mail display to drop down. If he was quick, he'd just have time to send the message to Rob before Mr

Lewin came out to check up on him.

Mitch knew that once Rob knew where to look, he could log into the *New York Times* archives from way over in Portsmouth as easily as Mitch had done from CyberSnax.

Mitch finished his brief message and clicked SEND. Maybe now that his friends could find out where the ship had been, they'd be able to figure out where that captive animal had come from.

'Mitch!'

'On my way, Mr Lewin,' Mitch called with a grin as he trotted across the floor of the café. He unlocked the door, ready for the first customers to walk in and 'Surf while they sip', as Mr Lewin liked to put it.

CyberSnax was open for business.

CHAPTER 6

Perth, Australia. 9 p.m.
Tom sat staring disconsolately at his computer screen. There hadn't been a single, solitary response to his cleverly worded message on the Net bulletin board. If Filefly was out there, either he hadn't logged in, or he wasn't biting.

Come on, sport, Tom thought impatiently. *Take the bait, can't you?*

He glared at the mail box in the bottom right hand corner of his screen.

```
MAIL: 0 MESSAGES WAITING
```

Dreams of trapping the elusive Filefly began to drift away. If there was one thing Tom wasn't very good at, it was hanging around *waiting.*

'OK, bug-face,' Tom murmured to himself. 'You just carry on playing hard to get. I've got other things to do, mate!'

He clicked into his mail log, where he had left Tamsyn's recent call for help, along with the two updates from Lauren and Mitch.

Maybe if he did some good detective work for

his friends, it would cheer him up a bit after his total failure with Filefly.

'Filefly!' Tom muttered under his breath as he pulled up the *New York Times* archive file that Mitch had mentioned. 'I'll give you *Filefly* if I do catch you. I'll swat you so good that you wouldn't be able to fly even if you had seats booked with Qantas!'

He read the article on the Stonewall Jay. It was interesting that the ship's home port was Sydney, but if Lauren was right about the animal being a tamarin, then Tom couldn't see any obvious connection between Southern Star Ltd and the appearance of a South American endangered animal in Portsmouth.

But that didn't mean that Tom wasn't ready and able to do some digging for himself.

'I'm not called Sherlock for nothing,' he said as he opened the special drawer that contained his own crime file. He had changed his user name to Sherlock when the long-promised home computer had finally appeared. Tom liked to think that he was at least as good a detective as Sherlock Holmes. Better, even – after all, in Holmes's day there hadn't been an Internet to help the famous private investigator solve crimes.

Tom took out his crime notebook and opened it to a clean page. He smiled to himself as he wrote a heading for the top of the new page.

The strange case of the vanishing monkey.

He sucked the end of his pen for a few moments, and then started to write.

Fact: Rare monkey on ship. Crew say they don't know it's there. True/False? Explanation: It's been smuggled on board. With or without help from crew?
Question: Why would someone smuggle a monkey on board a ship?
Answer:

His pen went back into his mouth. Good question! A thought struck him. One of the main sources of crime-busting information to which he was constantly returning was an Internet Crime section.

Part of this particular Crime site, Tom thought, might prove especially useful. It contained a series of files which explained and explored specific types of crime.

Tom scrolled down the screen until he came to S.

'That's the one,' he said, clicking on the word *Smuggling*. 'Now then, let's see if I can find something about animal smuggling.'

Manor House, Portsmouth. 1.30 p.m.

Tamsyn planned on spending a pleasant afternoon in the Charles Dickens Birthplace Museum in the town centre. Dickens was far and away her favourite author and she had been to the old house several times before, but she did like to revisit it and soak up the atmosphere at least once a year.

But first of all she had decided to make a brief detour up Portsdown Hill to see if Rob had received any messages from the others.

She marched up the tarmac pathway to the large house where Rob and his parents lived, and pressed the intercom.

'Who's there?' came Rob's tinny voice through the metal grille.

'Boo,' Tamsyn said with a grin.

'Sorry? What did you say?' came the reply.

'Rob, it's me, Tamsyn.'

'Oh. I thought you said "Boo".'

'I did. I said "Boo", so you could say, "Boo who?" And then I'd say, "Don't cry, it's only me." It's a joke!'

'It is?'

'Yes!' Tamsyn frowned at the intercom box. 'How come it always works when Josh does it?'

'Perhaps Josh is better at it than you are.' Tamsyn could hear Rob's stifled laughter.

'Oh, come on,' Tamsyn said, realizing Rob was making fun of her. 'Stop messing about and let me in, will you?'

The intercom buzzed and the front door clicked open. Tamsyn found Rob in his bedroom. His computer was on and she could see he was in the middle of typing something.

'Have any of the others replied?' she asked.

Rob nodded. 'It looks like Lauren has discovered what the animal was,' he said. 'And Mitch has come up with a whole lot of stuff about the ship and the people who own it.' He gestured towards the screen. 'I was just making some notes. Hold on a sec and I'll show you the stuff Lauren sent. There's a picture.'

Tamsyn sat down beside Rob as he clicked up Lauren's e-mail with the page of the Animals Unlimited CD-ROM attached.

'I thought Josh would be here,' said Tamsyn.

'He was,' Rob replied, 'but he had to meet someone in town.'

The screen changed.

'That's it!' Tamsyn breathed as she stared at the picture of the golden lion tamarin. 'That's *exactly* it.'

'Good,' said Rob. 'I hoped you'd say that. Now take a look at this.' He handed Tamsyn a sheet of paper. On it was printed the world map showing the route taken by the Stonewall Jay.

'I printed this out from the file Mitch told us about.'

Tamsyn slid her finger up the eastern side of the South American continent. 'It fits perfectly,' she said, tapping her fingertip just under the bulge of Brazil. She looked up at the page on the screen.

'That's where the golden lion tamarins live,' she said. 'According to what Lauren sent us, it's the *only* place they live! Our tamarin must have been smuggled aboard when the ship put in at Rio de Janeiro.' She made a grimace of disgust as she traced the Stonewall Jay's continuing journey. 'They stopped off at Caracas, then at Tampico in Mexico, New Orleans, Miami *and New York*!' she said angrily. 'That poor thing must have been cooped up in that crate for weeks and weeks!'

'Yeah, but *why*?' asked Rob. 'You said yourself the tamarin wasn't being treated like a pet. And judging by what it says about them on the CD-ROM, they'd make pretty ferocious pets, anyway.'

'Maybe this man thinks he'll be able to sell it to a zoo, or something?' Tamsyn said.

'That would be illegal,' Rob pointed out. 'I'm sure a zoo wouldn't buy an endangered animal off someone without asking a few questions first.'

'OK, so why else would someone try to illegally import an endangered animal into the country?' asked Tamsyn.

'We don't know he is trying to sneak it into this country,' said Rob. 'Apart from the fact that the RSPCA couldn't find it on board, we've got no proof that he took it off the ship.'

A sudden light ignited in Tamsyn's eyes. 'Wait a minute,' she breathed. 'With any luck, I think there may be a way of finding out whether he left the ship or not. Can I use your phone?'

'Of course,' Rob said. 'What's the plan?'

'You'll see!'

1.45 p.m.

Tamsyn perched on the arm of the couch in Rob's living room. Balanced on her knee was the leaflet that had been handed to them when they had bought their tickets to the Stonewall Jay tour. She had dialled the information number and was speaking to someone at the other end.

'I'm enquiring about the possibility of booking a cruise on the ship,' she said in as deep and adult-sounding a voice as she could manage.

'I'm afraid it's fully booked right through to Naples in Italy,' came the response. 'But I'll just check for cancellations. Ah, just a moment please. I think I may be able to help you after all.'

Tamsyn made a thumbs-up sign to Rob.

'Yes, I missed the entry – we do have one cabin available,' said the woman at the other end of the phone. 'One guest disembarked at Portsmouth. But you'll have to make your decision almost instantly. The Stonewall Jay is due to leave port tomorrow.'

'That's perfect,' Tamsyn said. 'I'll get back to you as soon as I can. Oh, one last thing. Er, this may sound a little strange, but I'm very superstitious about numbers. Would it be possible for you to tell me what number cabin I would be travelling in?'

'Certainly.' The woman sounded a little puzzled. Tamsyn could imagine her thinking: *We've got a right one here*! 'Yes, I can confirm that you would be travelling in cabin fifteen.'

Tamsyn flung her arm in the air and made a spinning ra-ra gesture with her fist. That was it! That was the number of the cabin where she'd seen the golden lion tamarin.

'Fifteen?' Tamsyn said into the phone. 'That's no good! Fifteen is the worst number in the world. I couldn't possibly travel in cabin number fifteen.'

'I beg your pardon?' came the startled response. 'Please, I can assure you—'

'I think I'll go by air, if it's all the same to you,' she said. 'Thanks for all your help.' She put the phone down.

'There you go,' she said to Rob, her eyes shining with triumph. 'He left the ship. I knew it! He's brought the tamarin into Britain *illegally*. Now, all we need to do is find out where he's taken it, and alert the police.'

Rob looked at her. 'That's *all*?' he said. 'Tamsyn, he's had days – he could be anywhere. How on earth are we going to find him?'

'I'll think of something,' Tamsyn said with determination. She jumped up. 'And as I do all my best thinking while I'm walking, I'll see you later.'

Rob gazed after Tamsyn as she strode down the pathway. He smiled quietly to himself as he closed the front door. One thing was for sure: once she got her teeth into a problem, she was harder to unclamp than a bulldog with lockjaw. If anyone could find that animal, then it was Tamsyn.

CHAPTER 7

Tricorn Market, Portsmouth. 2 p.m.

Josh was sitting at a window table in a small café that looked out on to the Tricorn Street Market. People were bustling about outside like ants, moving from stall to stall as they did their afternoon shopping.

Josh had finished his sandwich twenty minutes ago, and had just extracted the last molten-ice slurp from his Coke. Ritchie was late.

They had arranged to meet at half past one for a lunchtime snack, before going to Ritchie's house for an afternoon session on his computer. But Ritchie was now over half an hour late.

Josh sank his chin in his hand. Now that he thought about it, Ritchie had always been one of those people who seemed totally incapable of getting anywhere on time.

Then Josh saw Ritchie's head bobbing through the crowds that filled the space between the market stalls.

At last!

Ritchie slid into the seat opposite.

'Hello. Been waiting long?' he asked.

'Only half an hour or so,' Josh said drily. 'Where were you?'

Ritchie grinned. 'I must have lost track of the time. How about a doughnut and a Coke, then?'

Josh started to tell Ritchie about the attempts that he and the others were making to pull together some information about the animal that Tamsyn had seen.

Ritchie didn't seem in the least bit interested until the point where Josh mentioned the United States Naval site that they hadn't been able to get into.

Josh waved the remains of his doughnut dismissively as he spoke. 'Not that it mattered,' he said. 'It didn't look like the markings on the crate would lead us anywhere.'

Then Ritchie said something that stopped Josh in his tracks.

'Those sorts of sites are easy enough to get into, if you know the way,' Ritchie said casually.

Josh swallowed and frowned at his friend. 'How?'

'There are plenty of ways,' Ritchie said.

'Are you talking about *hacking* into them?' Josh asked.

Ritchie looked at him without expression for a few moments, then grinned. 'Maybe.'

'*Maybe*?' said Josh. 'How else do you get through a screen that says "Access denied"?'

Ritchie shrugged, but didn't reply.

Fingernails rattled on the window. The two

boys turned at the sound and saw Tamsyn standing outside.

Josh waved for her to come in.

Tamsyn looked questioningly at Josh's friend.

'This is Ritchie. We went to primary school
together,' Josh told Tamsyn. 'He's just back from
Australia.'

'Oh, right.' Tamsyn smiled at Ritchie. 'Hi.' She
shoved in next to Josh to tell him the latest news.

'I told Rob I'd come up with a brilliant plan for
tracking down our tamarin smuggler,' Tamsyn
said. 'But, so far, I haven't had a single idea. Like
Rob said – he could have taken the animal
anywhere by now.'

Josh sighed. 'That's a real drag,' he said.
'There's no way of finding out *where* he's gone.'

'There is if he uses a credit card or a cash card,'
Ritchie said.

The two friends looked at him.

'What do you mean?' Tamsyn asked. 'How
would that help?'

'All you have to do is get into the bank system
or the credit card system,' Ritchie said. 'Then you
can see where the bloke has been using his credit
card or taking cash out. Easy! The police do it all
the time when they're trying to track people
down.'

'Excuse me,' Tamsyn said, giving Ritchie a hard
look, 'I think you'll find they're not the sort of
systems you can just log into when you feel like
it.'

'Oh, really?' Ritchie said with a cocky smile that

Tamsyn found rather irritating. 'If you say so. I'm sure you know more about these things than I do.'

'Meaning what, exactly?' Tamsyn asked sharply.

'Meaning that all those blocking devices are only there to stop idiots getting in,' Ritchie said. 'Anyone with half a brain cell can work out ways to get through.'

'If you're talking about what I *think* you're talking about, it's *illegal*,' said Tamsyn. 'People get put into prison for *computer hacking*.'

'The stupid ones do,' Ritchie said casually. 'Anyway, *hacking* is breaking into files to steal stuff. There's no harm in taking a *look* at a couple of files.'

'And you know how to do that, do you?' asked Tamsyn.

'I might be able to help you out.'

Tamsyn shook her head. 'I don't think so, thanks all the same.' She got up. 'I must go.' She gave Ritchie a very frosty smile. 'Nice meeting you,' she said, sounding like she meant the exact opposite. She gave Josh an expressive look and then headed for the door.

Ritchie was silent until Tamsyn had left the café.

'She's a bit uptight, isn't she?' he said.

'Not especially,' Josh said. 'She just doesn't like the idea of breaking the law, that's all.'

'Sheesh,' Ritchie said. 'Don't you people ever have any *fun*? Oh, forget I mentioned it. Are we going back to my place, or what? Did you bring those games you were talking about?'

That morning Josh had borrowed a couple of brand new computer games from Rob. From what he could make out, Ritchie had no games at all. Rob's parents owned GAMEZONE, a company which produced state-of-the-art computer games, so he always had the latest thing.

Josh nodded.

They left the café and headed off towards Ritchie's house. As they walked along, Josh found himself wondering uneasily exactly what Ritchie Moore meant when he talked about having fun.

Perth, Australia. 10.11 p.m.

Mr Peterson's head appeared around the door of the room where the computer was set up. Tom was busy reading his Crime files.

'Hey sport, have you taken a gander at the *time*, recently?' his father called.

Tom glanced at the clock display. 22:11.

'Strewth!'

Tom had been so absorbed in his investigations that he hadn't realized how the evening had been speeding by.

'You've got school tomorrow, Tom,' Mr Peterson said, as he came into the room. 'Don't you think you should shut up shop now before your mother goes on the warpath?' He leaned over Tom's shoulder. 'What's got you square-eyed tonight, anyway?'

Tom quickly filled his father in on his attempts

to help Tamsyn and the others in Portsmouth.

The crime file had thrown up some interesting stuff on smuggling – but nothing that shed much light on the problem in hand.

'The thing to bear in mind,' said Mr Peterson, 'is that there is nearly always a Mister Big behind any smuggling ring. Find him, and you can break the whole case wide open. From what you said, it sounds like the guy with the tamarin was probably just a courier. If your mate Tamsyn really wants to get anywhere, she needs to find out who Mister Big is.'

He reached over Tom's shoulder and pressed the EXIT key. 'And if I were you, I'd strongly recommend she goes straight to the *police*, OK?'

'Yeah, but I just need to—'

'Tomorrow, Tom!'

'Well, yeah, but—'

'Do you want me to call your mum?'

'No, thanks,' said Tom, bowing to the inevitable. 'I'm out of here!'

'And when you do get through to Tamsyn,' his father called out after him, 'you make sure you warn her that smugglers are a dangerous bunch of people. She should go to the police, right? Otherwise, she could find herself in bad trouble. *Very* bad trouble!'

Manor House, Portsmouth.
Thursday 24th February, 9.03 a.m.
Tamsyn rang the buzzer on Rob's front door at a

few minutes past nine the following morning. 'I've had an idea,' she said as he let her in. 'I need to use your computer.'

'Help yourself,' Rob said as he followed her into his room. 'What sort of idea is it?'

'Well, we may not be able to track the man down,' she explained, 'but I thought we might be able to trace the *animal*.'

'So, what are you planning on doing?'

'I need to find any Internet web sites that are based in this country, and which have anything to do with exotic animals,' Tamsyn said. 'I know we can't expect to trace the tamarin now, but if we could alert vets and zoos and people like that all over the country, then they'll be on the lookout for it. ' As she spoke, she moved the mouse around on its mat and clicked to move from menu to menu.

'I know who you should look for,' Rob said. 'See if that zoo just outside town has a site. The Van Meer Animal Sanctuary.'

A wide grin stretched across Tamsyn's face. 'Of course!' she said. 'I hadn't even thought about them. Brilliant!'

The Van Meer Animal Sanctuary was a wildlife park situated out in the countryside north-west of Portsmouth. It was only a short bus-ride away and Tamsyn had been there once before.

It was in the grounds of an old manor house, and was owned and run by a man named Don Van Meer – a foreign millionaire who had settled in Hampshire a few years back. Tamsyn remembered seeing Van Meer himself showing some important visitors round the zoo. An attendant had pointed him out to her and said he was very 'hands-on'.

Now that Tamsyn thought about it, contacting the Sanctuary was a brilliant idea. She was convinced that Mr Van Meer would be as incensed as she was when he learned that someone was trying to bring such a rare and endangered species of animal into the country.

A person like Don Van Meer could prove to be the exact ally she needed.

'Bingo!' Tamsyn shrieked a minute or so later. 'They *have* got a web site!' As she clicked on the link to take her there, Tamsyn finally felt that she was getting somewhere. She watched as the screen changed.

'OK,' Tasmyn said as she clicked into e-mail. 'Let's see where this gets us.' She grinned round at Rob and then started to type her message to the Sanctuary.

CHAPTER 8

Ritchie's house, Portsmouth. 11 a.m.

The computer screen flashed red and white and brilliant yellow as Ritchie's space freighter collided with an asteroid and splintered into a thousand spinning pieces.

'Hey, careful!' Josh said as Ritchie flung the control pad onto the floor. 'You'll be sorry if you break that.'

'It's a stupid game, anyway,' said Ritchie. 'A stupid, boring game for stupid, boring nerds.'

'Actually, it's dead good if you could be bothered to learn the rules and pay attention,' Josh said.

The truth was that Josh was rapidly losing patience with Ritchie. He had spent a couple of hours yesterday afternoon trying to get Ritchie interested in *Jungle Fever*, without much luck. The problem was becoming obvious: Ritchie *hated* losing; but he wasn't prepared to put any effort into learning to play the games properly and avoid being beaten.

Josh picked up the control pad, which seemed none the worse for its ill-treatment.

'Let me show you,' he said as he keyed *Alpha Primus* in for a new game. 'The trick is to steer around behind the asteroids, get it? Otherwise they just crunch straight into you.'

Josh expertly manipulated the joystick and the huge stellar freighter nipped deftly around a black hole, cleverly avoided an entire asteroid swarm and ducked out of the way of a passing comet.

'See?' Josh said. 'It's really good if you pay attention to what you're doing and think a bit. Easy-peasy, in fact, and – oh, blimey!' The screen flashed a rainbow of exploding colours as Josh's freighter crashed into the dark side of Neptune. 'Oops!'

Ritchie gave him a stony look. 'What's the point?' he said.

'Eh? What do you mean?'

Ritchie waved at the screen. 'Games!' he said. 'These stupid games. What's the point?'

Josh didn't quite know what to say. If a person needed to ask what the point of games was, what *could* you say?

'OK,' Josh sighed, pressing the EXIT button. 'I give up. If you don't like 'em, you don't like 'em.' He gave Ritchie a hopeful smile. 'Fancy a quick surf around the Net, then? See what we can find?'

'I'll tell you what,' Ritchie said. 'You've been showing me how to play your games.' He grinned. 'Maybe now I can show you one of the games I like to play.'

'OK,' Josh said. 'If you like.'

'Can you remember the letters and numbers that led you to that system you couldn't get into – the one where you were denied access?'

'Yes. Why?'

'Tell them to me,' Ritchie said.

Josh hesitated for a few moments before giving Ritchie the list of letters and numbers that had brought them up to the blank wall of the United States Navy system.

Ritchie scribbled them down on a scrap of paper.

'What are you going to do?' Josh asked.

'You'll see.'

Ritchie's fingers played over the keyboard.

'Let's find an interesting web site,' he said.

A few seconds later a new screen appeared.

'It's a hackers' newsgroup,' Josh said.

'Got it in one,' said Ritchie. 'It's the best info exchange I've ever come across. They keep moving about on the Net so as not to get closed down, but us regular users can always find them.'

Ritchie sped down a list on the screen.

'Gotcha!' He halted the page and moved the cursor on to a line which Josh could see read:

```
MILITARY RELATED PASSWORDS
```

'Ritchie! What on earth are you doing?'

'Keep your socks on – I'm just going to take a look.'

Josh watched the screen as Ritchie typed. His friend's pale face was darkly reflected in the glass. Ritchie was smiling. Josh didn't much like that smile.

A familiar, stark screen appeared.

U.S. NAVAL SECURITY PERSONNEL ONLY

ACCESS DENIED

'We'll see about that,' Ritchie murmured as he continued to type.

'Ritchie!'

Ritchie frowned at him. 'Look, if *I* can get through this, how secret can it be?'

Josh didn't reply.

Ritchie tapped ENTER.

Josh could hardly believe his eyes.

'That's it then,' said Josh, looking at the flashing screen. 'We can't search any further.'

'Oh yes you can,' said his friend. 'If you know how.'

Ritchie leaned over the keyboard and typed.

'That did the trick,' Ritchie said. 'We're in!' He glanced round at Josh and his grin faded as he saw the expression on his friend's face. 'What's up with you?'

'Are you completely out of your mind?' Josh said. 'Hacking is totally uncool, Ritchie. I don't want anything to do with this.'

'Oh, don't be such a weed,' Ritchie said, turning back to the screen. 'This is a load more fun than those stupid games of yours.'

Chair legs scraped as Josh stood up.

Ritchie looked up at him. 'Where are you going?'

'Home,' Josh snapped. 'Right now. Unless you exit out of there.'

'You're kidding?'

'No,' Josh said. 'I'm not kidding.'

Ritchie shrugged and turned back to the screen.

'I'll see you around then,' he said.

Josh gave it one final try. 'Look, Ritchie. I know you think this is just a laugh, but it isn't. You could get into really serious trouble with this stuff.'

'How?' Ritchie said, fixing Josh with his pale eyes. 'Are you going to tell on me?'

'Of course not, you idiot! But think about what you're doing, Ritchie. Think about what might happen when you get caught.'

Ritchie turned away. 'You know something,

Josh, you've got really boring over the last three years.'

Josh didn't reply. He walked out of Ritchie's bedroom and down the stairs to the front door.

If Ritchie wanted to act like a complete moron, that was his lookout, but he'd be doing it on his own.

Manor House, Portsmouth. 11.15 a.m.

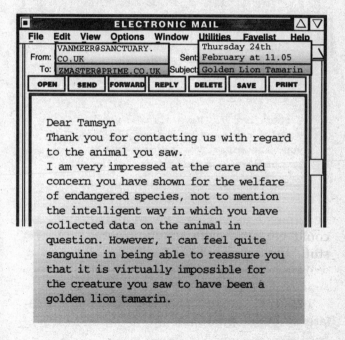

'Huh! Says you!' Tamsyn mumbled to herself

as she read the response that had come through from the Animal Sanctuary.

'He must know what he's talking about,' Rob said.

'Yeah, and I know what I saw!'

Tasmyn carried on reading from the screen.

As you know, vigorous restrictions on
the capture and exportation of golden
lion tamarins came into force some time
ago, and I can assure you that this
law is very strictly observed by all
relevant international enforcement
agencies. It would, therefore, be
totally impossible for anyone to
successfully import such a high-profile
animal into this country.

I feel that you have allowed your
genuine concerns to run away with
you. The animal you saw was in all
probability something quite different.

Tasmyn stared at the screen. 'What a cheek,' she said. 'That lot just means he thinks I was seeing things!'

'He is an expert,' Rob pointed out.

'Humph!' snorted Tasmyn. 'I'm not particularly *sanguine* about that!'

> May I suggest that you saw a macaque or possibly a langur? These animals are often kept perfectly legitimately as pets, and are in no way harmed by the experience. Nor are they endangered.
>
> Thank you for your concern.
>
> D. Van Meer
> The Van Meer Animal Sanctuary

Mail:

Tamsyn slumped back in the chair, her forehead knitted in a deep frown, and her arms folded crossly as she glowered at the message.

'Well?' asked Rob.

Tamsyn shook her head. 'He's wrong,' she said adamantly. 'I know what I saw.'

'At least check out what macaques and langurs look like, Tamsyn,' Rob said. 'You never know, you might—'

'I might have jumped to conclusions?' Tamsyn broke in. 'Is that what you think?'

'Not at all,' Rob said calmly. 'I was going to say, you might want to take another look, now you've got a second opinion.'

'OK,' said Tamsyn. 'I'll *look*. But I'm not convinced. And I can't say I'm particularly impressed by Mr Van Meer. I expected him to show a lot more concern than that.'

'He could be right, though,' Rob said.

Tamsyn shot him a look but said nothing.

She was far from convinced that it was *imposs-ible* for her to have seen a golden lion tamarin. *Very* far from convinced.

CHAPTER 9

New York, USA. 7.30 a.m.

Mitch whistled tunelessly between his teeth as his fingers played over the computer keyboard. He had to finish the e-mail message and get it sent off in the next couple of minutes, otherwise Mr Lewin would be on his case again.

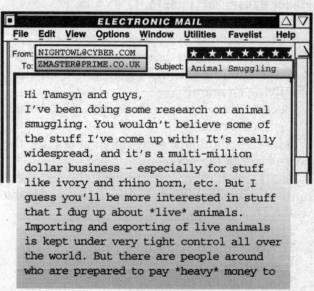

```
┌─────────────────────────────────────────────┐
│ ■        ELECTRONIC MAIL            △ ▽       │
│ File  Edit  View  Options  Window  Utilities  Favelist  Help │
│ ┌─────────────────────┐  ┌★★★★★★★★┐          │
│ From: NIGHTOWL@CYBER.COM  └────────────┘      │
│ To: ZMASTER@PRIME.CO.UK   Subject: Animal Smuggling │
│                                               │
│   Hi Tamsyn and guys,                         │
│   I've been doing some research on animal     │
│   smuggling. You wouldn't believe some of     │
│   the stuff I've come up with! It's really    │
│   widespread, and it's a multi-million        │
│   dollar business - especially for stuff      │
│   like ivory and rhino horn, etc. But I       │
│   guess you'll be more interested in stuff    │
│   that I dug up about *live* animals.         │
│   Importing and exporting of live animals     │
│   is kept under very tight control all over   │
│   the world. But there are people around      │
│   who are prepared to pay *heavy* money to    │
└─────────────────────────────────────────────┘
```

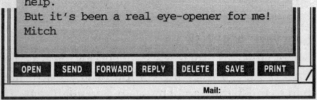

get their hands on particular species.
I guess that a golden lion tamarin would
be traded because it's so rare. It's kind
of like stealing a famous painting
(remember?). You couldn't ever show it to
anyone, but you could gloat over it in
private. If you were a total basket case.
I'm not sure how much this is going to
help.
But it's been a real eye-opener for me!
Mitch

| OPEN | SEND | FORWARD | REPLY | DELETE | SAVE | PRINT |

Mail:

Manor House, Portsmouth. 12.45 p.m.

Rob and Tamsyn looked at one another. Mitch's e-mail had been an eye-opener for them too.

'I just can't believe how cruel people can be,' said Tamsyn. 'How could *anyone* cause suffering to a living creature?'

'Because there's loads of money in it,' Rob said.

'I still don't see—'

Tamsyn's thoughts were interrupted by the harsh buzz of the intercom.

Rob leaned over and pressed the left-hand button on the silver box which was attached to the wall by his bedroom door.

'Hello?'

'It's Josh,' came the metallic reply.

'Josh *who*?'

'Sorry, Rob, I'm not in the mood.'

Rob gave Tamsyn a concerned glance as he pressed the right-hand button to allow their friend into the house. That wasn't like Josh at all.

Josh walked in and gave them a weak smile.

'How's the great tamarin hunt going?' he asked.

'Not too good,' said Tamsyn. 'I thought I was on to something this morning. I got in touch with the Van Meer Animal Sanctuary. But apparently Mr Van Meer thinks I'm just some stupid idiot who wouldn't know a tamarin from a plate of tapioca pudding.' She looked at him. 'Anyway, what's bothering you?'

'Oh, nothing.'

Tamsyn frowned. 'Don't give me that,' she said. 'You've got the longest face I've ever seen.' She looked at him with a sudden sharpness in her eyes. 'Is it that pal of yours? That Ritchie?'

'What makes you say that?' Josh asked defensively.

'I thought so!' said Tamsyn. 'I didn't like the look of him from the moment I set eyes on him. What's he done?'

Josh sat on Rob's bed. 'He was never *like* this when I knew him before,' he said dejectedly.

'Like what?' Rob asked.

Josh made a helpless gesture. 'Like he is now.'

'This is to do with hacking, isn't it?' Tamsyn said. She turned to Rob. 'He was boasting yesterday about how easy it was to get into restricted files if you knew the way.'

'He wasn't just *boasting*,' Josh said. 'I was at his

house this morning. He broke through that *access denied* block like it was nothing.'

Rob looked at his friend.

'That was a pretty idiotic thing to do.'

'I *know*.'

'The police are really hot on catching hackers.'

'I know!'

'People get sent to prison!'

Josh glared at him. 'Rob, *I know, I know*,' he snapped.

'Sorry. I was only trying to help.'

'Sure,' Josh sighed. 'I wasn't having a go at you. It's Ritchie that I'm angry with. The problem is that he seems to be treating it all as some big joke.'

'Excuse me,' said Tamsyn. 'I don't know him, but it seemed to me as if he gets his kicks that way. If you want my advice, I'd steer well clear of him.'

'I think Tamsyn's right,' added Rob. 'Who needs that sort of grief? I mean, he's going to get caught eventually, no matter how clever he thinks he is.'

Josh lifted his head and looked from one to the other.

'He was my best mate,' he said.

'*Was* being the operative word,' Tasmyn said.

Josh shook his head. 'He must have met up with some weirdos in Australia,' he said. 'That'll be how he's learned all this hacking stuff. Look, if we have a chat with him and explain why it's such a rubbish thing to do, I reckon he'll see the light.'

'What do you mean, *we*?' said Tamsyn.

'I just thought that maybe if I invited him around here, we could *all* talk to him.'

'He's not touching my system,' Rob said adamantly.

'I can't just *dump* him,' Josh said. 'I've known him since we were little kids. He's OK, really.'

He looked from Tamsyn to Rob, but there was very little sympathy in either of their faces.

'OK,' he sighed. 'It's not your problem. But I'll give it one more go.' He stood up. 'I'm going to go back to his house and try and talk some sense into him.'

'If it was a friend of mine,' Tamsyn said, 'I'd try *knocking* the sense in. With a *mallet!*'

Josh gave a feeble half-smile as he went through the door.

'Good luck,' Rob called.

The front door closed with a rattle.

'He'll need it,' Tamsyn said. 'I don't often dislike people at first sight, but I really made an exception in Ritchie's case.'

Josh was determined not to abandon his old friend quite so easily. A bus from the end of Rob's road took him back into town.

He walked up the path to Ritchie's house and rang the bell.

He waited a while before ringing again.

There was no response.

Josh crouched and flicked the letter box open. 'Ritchie!' he called. 'Are you in there? It's Josh!'

But if Ritchie was in the house, he was lying low.

OK, thought Josh as he walked slowly back down the street, *I'll just have to try again tomorrow.*

From an upstairs window in Ritchie's house, a pair of unseen pale blue eyes watched Josh's retreat. A thin, mocking smile was on Ritchie's lips as he turned back to his computer.

Perth, Australia. 9 p.m.

'Mister Big,' Tom muttered to himself, as he navigated his way through the archive section of yet another Australian newspaper. 'Must find Mister Big.'

He had been searching all evening, for something which he could send off to Tamsyn to let them know he was on the case.

The section of his Crime file web site which covered smuggling had included a whole list of cross-references, both to other scientific and educational locations, and to news sites.

It was the news archives which had been holding Tom's attention ever since.

Typing *smuggling* into the search panel had narrowed the field down considerably, but Tom still found himself faced by page after page of headlines. They covered everything from million-dollar hauls of illegal drugs discovered hidden on cross-continental trucks, to a woman convicted of trying to sneak an American bullfrog into the country concealed in her handbag.

He needed to narrow the search even more and whipped the cursor down to the search panel again.

```
SEARCH FOR? Animal Smuggling

SEARCH RESULTS: Found 3 matches
```

Maybe now he'd find something useful.

CHAPTER 10

Ritchie's house, Portsmouth.
Friday 24th February, 10 a.m.

Josh was determined to do his best to clue Ritchie in on the consequences of hacking. Richie might think he was taking it all a bit too seriously – and maybe he was getting a bit uptight – but hacking was a serious subject, and Josh didn't want to see his old friend get into trouble. Yesterday there had been no reply at the house, despite the fact that Josh was quite convinced that Ritchie had been in there. This morning, Josh had a bit of luck.

As he walked up the short front path, the door opened unexpectedly and Ritchie's mother appeared. She was a small, pale, wispy woman with the same ginger hair and glassy blue eyes as her son.

'Hello there, Josh,' she said. 'Ritchie told me he'd got back in touch with you. Sorry I can't stop and chat, but I'm in a real rush. Ritchie's up in his room.'

'Thanks.' Josh smiled and waved as she headed off down the street.

His smile faded as he closed the front door behind himself and set off up the stairs.

Just as Mrs Moore had said, he found Ritchie bent over his computer. Ritchie turned on hearing Josh enter his room.

'I knew you'd come back,' he said. 'I just *knew* you wouldn't be able to resist it.'

Josh frowned. 'What's that supposed to mean?'

'Come off it,' Ritchie said, grinning. 'You want to know what I found out from that site, don't you? You can't kid me, Josh.'

'Actually,' Josh said, 'I came back to try and talk some sense into you.'

Ritchie laughed. 'Who made you my conscience all of a sudden?' He turned and his fingers skipped over the keyboard. The screen changed several times and then settled on a long list of some sort. Ritchie moved the cursor to about a third of the way down the list.

'I got sidetracked with something else after you had your little temper tantrum yesterday,' Ritchie said. 'I never found out what that code stood for.' He pushed his chair away from the desk. 'It's up to you, Josh. If you click the mouse, the page you want will appear on screen. If you're not interested, just press EXIT.'

Josh moved towards the screen.

Josh stared at the screen. One touch of the mouse and he may have the answer to Tamsyn's riddle.

Ritchie smiled as Josh hesitated.

'It's make-your-mind-up time,' he said.

'Oh, shut up, Ritchie!' Josh snapped. He brought his hand down on the mouse and clicked.

USNSS2050/733

```
Requisition order for two hundred cans
of corned beef for SS Stonewall Jay.

Order cleared by Lt. John Walker.
Quartermasters Offices, Atlantic City.
```

Josh burst out laughing.

'What's so funny?' Ritchie said, sliding his chair back in front of the screen.

'You are!' Josh chuckled. 'You went to all that trouble hacking into a secret file only to find out that the code was for a crate full of corned beef! That's priceless!' He went off into another peal of laughter.

Ritchie's eyes narrowed in annoyance. If there was one thing he hated above everything else, it was being laughed at. He stared at the screen for a few moments, then started to type.

'Now what?' Josh asked. 'Are you looking for some recipes about how to cook two hundred cans worth of corned beef?'

'Nope,' Ritchie said. 'The requisition is fifteen years old. I want to know ... Ah!' He looked round at Josh with the old gleam back in his eyes. 'I've just found their transactions database. The Stonewall Jay and everything on board it was sold to a company called—'

'Southern Star,' Josh interrupted. 'I already know that. They're Australian and they're run by some bloke called Perry McNab.' Josh grinned at Ritchie. 'Try telling me something I don't already know, Ritchie.' He waved a dismissive hand at the screen. 'You see? All that sneaky hacking and what have you actually come up with? Nothing! I always knew hacking was a stupid thing to do, but thanks to you, I now know it's a total waste of time and effort as well.'

'We'll see about that,' Ritchie said. 'You want to know some stuff you couldn't find out any other way? I'll show you some stuff!'

'Oh, no you won't,' Josh said. 'If you're too thick to know when to stop, that's your look-out, Ritchie. But you're on your own. If you change your mind and want to talk, I'll be in the café in Tricorn market for the next hour or so.' He turned his head as he was about to close the door behind himself. 'It's time you grew up a bit, Ritchie. Hacking is for nerds!'

*

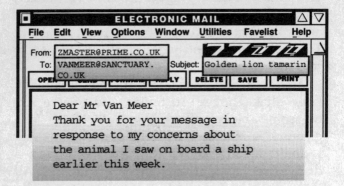

Dear Mr Van Meer
Thank you for your message in
response to my concerns about
the animal I saw on board a ship
earlier this week.

'Don't you want to specify which ship it was?'
asked Rob, looking over Tamsyn's shoulder as she
typed.

'It doesn't matter which ship,' said Tamsyn. 'I
never mentioned what ship it was before. And
don't interrupt. I'm thinking.'

She continued to type.

I have looked at pictures of langurs
and macaques. Neither of these are
anything like the animal I saw. It
was *definitely* a golden lion
tamarin. I think this animal has
been brought into the country
illegally because of its rarity
value.
All I ask is that you, please,
alert all contacts you have in this
country, and tell them to be on the
lookout for a golden lion tamarin. I
shall also be contacting other zoos

as well as vets and other animal
welfare organizations.
Yours, Tamsyn Smith

Mail:

'Okey-dokey,' Tamsyn said as she pressed
SEND. 'Let's see what he makes of that.'

10.55 a.m.

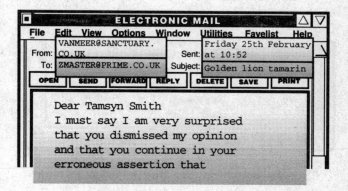

ELECTRONIC MAIL

File   Edit   View   Options   Window   Utilities   Favelist   Help

From: VANMEER@SANCTUARY.
CO.UK
To: ZMASTER@PRIME.CO.UK

Sent: Friday 25th February
at 10:52
Subject: Golden lion tamarin

OPEN   SEND   FORWARD   REPLY   DELETE   SAVE   PRINT

Dear Tamsyn Smith
I must say I am very surprised
that you dismissed my opinion
and that you continue in your
erroneous assertion that

'*Erroneous assertion*!' Tamsyn growled. 'What
does that bloke have for breakfast, Alphabetti
Spaghetti?'

the animal you saw was a golden
lion tamarin. It would be quite
impossible for such an animal to
be brought ashore, as the port
authorities would certainly
confiscate it.

'Well, *yes*,' Tamsyn said. 'I'm sure they *would*, if the bloke was stupid enough to march past them with it tucked under his arm! He must have hidden it, you big-headed fool!'

'Temper, temper!' cautioned Rob.

'We-*ell*!'

Even if you were correct, the
animal was certainly destined for a
country other than the UK. If there
was a tamarin aboard the Stonewall
Jay, it would be taken to one of
the Mediterranean ports. And as
the ship has now left Portsmouth,
I see no possible purpose in you
continuing with this campaign, and
I strongly urge you not to bother
people with pointless e-mails.
Yours, Don Van Meer

Mail:

Tamsyn sat staring at the message thoughtfully.

'I think that's what's known as telling you to shut up and shove off,' Rob said quietly.

'He'll be lucky,' Tamsyn said. 'There's something fishy going on here.'

'Like what?'

'Like … how did Van Meer know I saw the tamarin on board the Stonewall Jay?'

'I suppose he worked it out,' Rob said.

'Get out of it!' Tamsyn said. 'There are ships

coming and going all the time. And how come he knew that the Stonewall Jay had sailed, *and* where it was going next? How come he knew the Stonewall Jay was heading for the Mediterranean?'

'That's no big secret,' Rob said.

'I'm not suggesting it is,' said Tamsyn. 'But he'd have to find out, wouldn't he? So why did he bother? Look, I'm telling you, Rob, there's something really odd about this. And he's so insistent that I drop the whole thing. Why? What's his *problem*?'

'Well, one thing's for sure,' Rob said. 'It isn't something we're going to be able to find out by sitting here sending messages to him. The chances are he wouldn't even bother replying to another e-mail from you, anyway.'

'So, what can we do?' said Tamsyn.

'Easy,' Rob said. 'Get your coat, Tamsyn, we're going for a visit.'

'Eh? Where?'

Rob smiled. 'The Van Meer Animal Sanctuary,' he said as he headed for the door. 'Where else?'

Perth, Australia. 7.10 p.m. (UK time: 11.10 a.m.)
Tom was vaguely aware of the phone ringing in another part of the house as he sat over the computer that evening.

'You low-down, sneaky slimeball,' Tom whispered to himself as he read through the newspaper article for the second time. Bells had begun to ring during his initial readthrough of the second item of the three-item match his *animal smuggling* search had thrown up.

He had exited and gone into the *New York Times* archive file that Mitch had told everyone about. A rapid scan of *that* story had confirmed his suspicions.

The article in the Australian newspaper concerned a major smuggling ring that had been broken up about a decade ago. The ring had traded in the illegal export and import of animals for private collections on a global scale, netting millions of dollars before the police closed in on them. There was a 'Mr Big' and he had been caught and served two years in prison. On release, he had been free to leave the country.

There was no new information about him on file, but there was a suggestion that, as he had contacts in South America, he may have gone there.

But it wasn't so much where 'Mr Big' had gone that interested Tom. It was more to do with where he had worked before he had vanished. The company had been completely cleared of any involvement in the man's illegal activities, but it was still very intriguing.

The man had worked for Southern Star Limited – the company who *owned* the Stonewall Jay!

'Well, guys,' Tom said as he started typing an

e-mail to his friends in Portsmouth. 'This is going to give you something to think about, that's for sure!'

He heard his father's voice out in the hall.

'I'll be as quick as I can,' Mr Peterson was calling to Tom's mother. 'That call was from the station. Filefly is up to his old tricks again, and this time they reckon we'll cook him like a burger on a barbie!'

The front door slammed.

Tom grinned to himself. Wow! What a family!

CHAPTER 11

Tricorn Market, Portsmouth. 11.15 a.m.

Josh sat and stared sullenly out of the café window. He had been there, brooding over an empty plate, for nearly an hour. Ritchie wasn't going to come.

The same thought kept rolling around Josh's head. *I shouldn't have walked out. I should have stayed there until I convinced him.*

He had genuinely believed that his parting words to Ritchie would bring home to his wayward friend the consequences of all that stupid hacking. *You keep on doing that and I'm out of here – permanently!*

So much for that bright idea!

Josh shook his head, annoyed that he had failed to get through to Ritchie. He had decided to leave when the café door chimed open and Ritchie walked in.

Ritchie slid into a seat opposite Josh.

Josh smiled at him in relief. 'Fancy a Coke and a doughnut?'

'I've found out some stuff that you're really going to want to know,' Ritchie said.

Josh frowned at him. 'You've been at it again, haven't you?'

Ritchie leaned over the table. 'You wanted to know stuff that you couldn't find out yourself,' he said softly. 'Well, I've got it. I've found the link between the Stonewall Jay and Southern Star and your pal's monkey.' Ritchie leaned back and folded his arms. 'Wanna know what I found out, then, or what?'

'Let me guess,' Josh said with heavy sarcasm. 'You've found out that tamarins eat corned beef and like to go on long sea voyages. Am I getting warm?'

Ritchie smiled coldly. 'Funn-ee,' he said. 'Now, if you want me to tell you what I know, you're going to have to say *please*.'

Josh jerked forward. 'Now listen, Ritchie: watch my lips very carefully and pay attention. If you want to hack into secure files – well, fine. It's stupid, but it's up to you. And I'm not interested.'

'Oh, right! And I suppose you weren't interested earlier when you did your own bit of hacking. That mouse didn't click itself, Josh, so you can stop trying to be all superior.'

'You're right,' Josh said. 'I shouldn't have done that. But I'm not trying to be superior, Ritchie, I'm just trying to warn you that you're totally, absolutely and completely *guaranteed* to get caught!'

'They haven't caught me yet,' Ritchie said quietly. 'I've been doing it for ages.' A smirk spread across his face. 'I even broke into the police computer back in Australia, and they still didn't have a clue how to track me down. I even gave them a user name – Filefly – and they still couldn't find me. I've been back into their computer this morning – that was where I got the first clue about the tamarin.'

'I don't want to know,' Josh hissed. 'You're crackers, Ritchie. They'll *get* you, you idiot!'

Ritchie stared at Josh. 'You really don't want to know what I found out? Seriously?'

'Put out the flags!' Josh said. 'He's finally twigged! No, Ritchie, I *don't* want to know anything you found out *illegally*.'

There was a long silence between them.

'You don't want to be friends with me unless I stop, right?' Ritchie said softly. 'Is that it?'

Josh shrugged.

'OK,' Ritchie said. 'You win. I think you're an idiot, but you win.'

'Really?'

Ritchie nodded. 'Wanna come back to my place? Maybe we can find some games on the Net?'

Josh let out a long breath of relief. 'Yeah. Come on.'

During the walk back to Ritchie's home, Josh told him about a few of the adventures he'd had with his friends in the past.

'Maybe we could all get together and …' Josh's

voice faded. They had just rounded the corner into Ritchie's street. Ritchie had stopped dead in his tracks.

There was a police car outside his house. Two police officers stood on the pavement and a plain-clothed woman was just coming back down the path.

Josh looked at Ritchie. All the colour had drained from his face. Without a word being spoken, they both knew exactly what that police car was doing there. Filefly had finally been tracked down.

'Ritchie,' Josh murmured. 'If I can ...'

Ritchie glanced at him and a faint, wintry smile flickered across his lips. 'Looks like I'm not as clever as I thought,' he said.

'I'll come with you.'

'No, you won't. This is nothing to do with you, Josh.'

'But ...'

'Just *go* will you? Please! Just *go*!'

Josh watched for a few seconds as Ritchie walked steadily along the street to meet his fate. The plain-clothes policewoman came forwards.

Faintly, Josh heard her words: 'Are you Ritchie Moore?' Ritchie nodded. 'I think you know why we're here, Ritchie.'

Josh turned and walked away. There was nothing he could do for Ritchie. Not a single thing.

*

The Uan Meer Animal Sanctuary, Portsmouth.
12.15 p.m.

'All we can do,' Rob said as Tamsyn pushed his wheelchair towards the main entrance of the Animal Sanctuary, 'is have a good look around. Try and spot something that looks vaguely dodgy. See if we can chat to a keeper or someone who works here.'

'We might even get to have a word with Van Meer himself,' Tamsyn said. 'There are a few questions I'd like to ask him if I get the chance.'

'You're not going to start a row, are you?' Rob asked. 'If you have a go at him, he'll just clam up and sling you out.'

'Yes, yes, I know. I'm not daft.'

The entrance to the Sanctuary was at the end of a long, winding, tree-lined road. There were black iron gates to allow access for cars, and a smaller side entrance with a booth, where visitors paid the small entry fee.

Just as Tamsyn turned to hand a guide-leaflet to Rob, a car pulled up inside the gates and the horn tooted.

The woman in the ticket booth went to open the gates to let the car out.

Tamsyn glanced disinterestedly into the car.

'Careful!' Rob said as the change from the ticket money fell from Tamsyn's hand and rolled on the tarmac. 'If you're chucking it away, chuck it in my direction.' He looked up. Her face was white. She seemed almost stiff with shock.

'Tamsyn?'

The car sped away down the long, winding road and the woman closed the gates.

Tamsyn crouched and picked the coins up. She stood up, still staring after the vanished car.

'Excuse me,' she said in a choky kind of voice as the woman passed her on the way back to the booth. 'Who was that?'

'He works for Mr Van Meer sometimes,' the woman said casually. 'His name's Treeves, I think.'

'Do you know why he was here?'

'Search me,' said the woman. She snapped the little door to her booth closed. 'No one tells me nuffin',' she said with a smile.

Rob moved out of the way of a couple of people who wanted to get into the Sanctuary.

'Tamsyn? What's up?'

His friend seemed to pull herself together. She walked away from the entrance towards a quieter corner.

'The man driving that car,' she said in a low voice, as if scared she might be overheard. 'It was the man from the ship. The man with the tamarin.'

Rob looked searchingly into her face. 'Certain?'

Tamsyn nodded. 'Greasy black hair, nasty little caterpillar moustache and big fat slobby chops. It was him, all right.'

'That's the connection,' Rob said. 'I'll bet you

anything you like, your tamarin is right *here*!'

Tamsyn nodded. 'Let's go and look,' she said grimly.

There were several enclosures that housed monkeys, but the two friends spent twenty minutes scouring the place without catching a glimpse of so much as a single golden hair of a tamarin.

'Wait a minute,' said Tamsyn. 'We're doing this all wrong.'

'How's that?' Rob asked.

'Well, the tamarin was brought here illegally, right? So he's not going to have it out on open display, is he? He'll have it tucked away somewhere secret.'

'Any ideas?'

'Not really,' she said. 'But I reckon our best bet is to go and take a look at the house. Maybe it'll be in there somewhere – caged up in a room where he thinks no one will find it.'

Rob nodded. 'Let's go for it,' he said.

They headed towards the large old red-brick house where the Sanctuary's offices were situated. The house stood in the centre of the grounds like the hub of a wheel. All around it were the cages and compounds and paddocks, separated by gravel paths and screens of bushes and tall trees.

Stretching out to one side of the house, behind a row of trees, was a modern-looking annexe. Tamsyn assumed it must be some sort of storage area because there wasn't a single window in the whole long stretch of yellow brickwork.

Through a window of the house, they could see a tall, rugged-faced, grey-haired man in an office, talking on the telephone.

'That's him,' Tamsyn said. 'That's Van Meer.' She frowned. 'It looks like the only way into the house is through that office,' she said. 'We've got to get him out of the way somehow.'

'Leave him to me,' Rob said. 'I'll create a diversion. Be ready to dive in there the moment he comes out.'

'What are you going to do?'

'I'm going to have a fall,' Rob said. 'It's OK, I can do it without hurting myself. But I'll make a big fuss, so they have to fetch Van Meer.'

'Be careful,' Tamsyn said as Rob moved away and disappeared around a clump of bushes.

She positioned herself out of sight and waited.

A minute later there were shouts from a little way off. A young keeper came haring along the path.

'Mr Van Meer!' she yelled, as she stuck her head in through the office door. 'There's been an accident. A boy fell out of his wheelchair. I think he's hurt.'

Van Meer and the woman ran back the way Rob had gone. The diversion was working!

Quick as lightning, Tamsyn slid into the empty

office. The manor house was big and she wasn't going to have time to search the whole place before Van Meer returned.

A computer screen was lit up on a large desk against one wall. Glancing nervously over her shoulder, Tamsyn ran over to it.

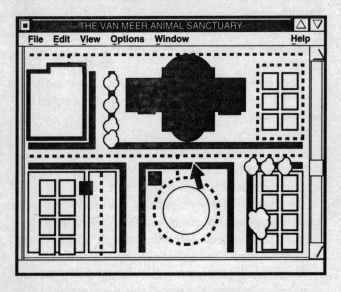

Tamsyn moved the cursor onto the house icon and clicked. A list of titles came up in one corner of the screen.

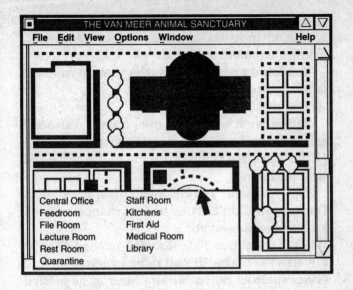

Central Office   Staff Room
Feedroom   Kitchens
File Room   First Aid
Lecture Room   Medical Room
Rest Room   Library
Quarantine

For a moment, Tamsyn let the cursor hover over *Medical Room*. But then she moved it down and clicked on the area marked *Quarantine*. She couldn't have said why, but something seemed to almost *draw* her to that title.

She stared at the screen that dropped down.

12.45 p.m.
'I'm OK,' Rob gasped as several pairs of hands helped him back into his wheelchair. 'Really! I'm not hurt.'

'Are you on your own, lad?' Van Meer asked. Rob was surprised to hear that the grey-haired man had a strong Australian accent.

'Er … yes …'

'What happened to that girl you came in with?' asked a woman's voice.

Rob looked round. It was the woman from the ticket booth.

'Oh, she … er … she's gone.'

'I think we'd better call your parents,' Van Meer said as he took a firm grip on the handles of Rob's chair. 'You'd best come with me to the office and wait for them.'

'No,' Rob said. 'I'm OK, really.' It was too soon. Tamsyn wouldn't have had a chance to look around the house yet.

'We'll see about that.' Rob was pushed straight towards the house. 'It's all right, everyone, it's all under control,' called Mr Van Meer as he guided Rob along the path to the office.

'I'm fine, really,' Rob said.

'I still think I should call your parents and explain what happened,' Van Meer said. 'And you'll need to help me fill in an accident report card for the Health and Safety people.'

Van Meer pushed Rob into the office. Tamsyn was nowhere to be seen. Rob only hoped that she'd stay that way!

Van Meer was about to pick up the telephone when he glanced at the computer screen. Rob couldn't see the screen, but he saw a look of shock sweep over Van Meer's face.

Then Van Meer stared at Rob with horribly narrowed eyes.

'Where's the girl you were with?' he hissed.

'Sorry?' *Play it dumb, Rob!*

Van Meer stalked over to the office door and turned the key. Then he quickly lowered the blinds over the window.

He turned Rob to face him, leaning low over the chair so his angry face was only inches away from Rob's.

'I think you'd better tell me what you're playing at, boy, before I have to get rough.'

Rob swallowed as he stared up into the man's cold eyes. Things had suddenly got way out of hand!

Manor House, Portsmouth. 11.40 a.m.

Rob's mother was just leaving Manor House when Josh arrived. She told Josh that she'd found a note from Rob, saying that he'd gone to the Van Meer Animal Sanctuary with Tamsyn. There was no mention of why.

'Can I take a quick look at his PC?' Josh asked.

'Of course you can,' she said. 'I've got to go. You can let yourself out, can't you?'

'Yes. Thanks.'

The front door slammed.

Josh booted up the computer and clicked his way into Rob's e-mail application. He read the last message from Van Meer. Even without knowing exactly what Tamsyn had said to him, it was pretty obvious to Josh that Van Meer was warning her off.

Josh heard the growl of Mrs Zanelli's car fade into the distance.

It was while he was puzzling over why Van Meer should be so insistent that Tamsyn drop the tamarin business, that he noticed another message was waiting.

Josh opened it.

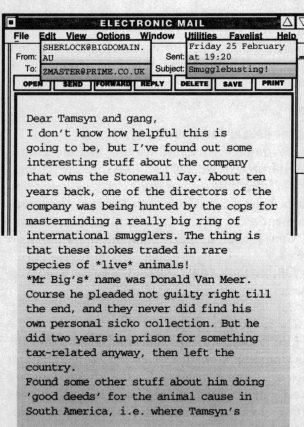

```
┌─┬──────────────────────────────────────┬─┬─┐
│■│         ELECTRONIC MAIL              │△│▽│
├─┴──────────────────────────────────────┴─┴─┤
│ File  Edit  View  Options  Window  Utilities  Favelist  Help │
│        ┌──────────────────┐      ┌───────────────┐ │
│        │ SHERLOCK@BIGDOMAIN.│     │ Friday 25 February│ │
│ From:  │ AU               │ Sent:│ at 19:20        │ │
│ To:    │ ZMASTER@PRIME.CO.UK│ Subject:│ Smugglebusting!│ │
│        └──────────────────┘      └───────────────┘ │
│ OPEN   SEND  FORWARD  REPLY   DELETE   SAVE   PRINT │
├─────────────────────────────────────────────┤
│                                             │
│   Dear Tamsyn and gang,                     │
│   I don't know how helpful this is          │
│   going to be, but I've found out some      │
│   interesting stuff about the company       │
│   that owns the Stonewall Jay. About ten    │
│   years back, one of the directors of the   │
│   company was being hunted by the cops for  │
│   masterminding a really big ring of        │
│   international smugglers. The thing is      │
│   that these blokes traded in rare          │
│   species of *live* animals!                │
│   *Mr Big's* name was Donald Van Meer.      │
│   Course he pleaded not guilty right till   │
│   the end, and they never did find his      │
│   own personal sicko collection. But he     │
│   did two years in prison for something     │
│   tax-related anyway, then left the         │
│   country.                                  │
│   Found some other stuff about him doing    │
│   'good deeds' for the animal cause in      │
│   South America, i.e. where Tamsyn's        │
└─────────────────────────────────────────────┘
```

tamarins come from! Pretty darned big
coincidence, eh, guys?
I reckon this Donald Van Meer might just
be up to his old tricks again, don't
y'think? Old habits die hard? Watch
out, anyway.
Hope this will be useful.
Tom

ZZZZ   Mail:

CHAPTER 12

The Van Meer Animal Sanctuary, Portsmouth. 12.40 p.m.

Tamsyn crept along a narrow white corridor. There were no windows, and no doors, except for a silver one that barred her way down at the end of the bleached tunnel. She knew from her memory of the way the house was laid out that she was heading towards the yellow-brick annexe. She glanced back at the door through which she had just come, the door to Mr Van Meer's office. She had left it slightly ajar. If there was anyone in this part of the house, she didn't want a closed door between her and an escape route.

As she approached the silver door, she saw a metal box which took the place of a normal lock. Tamsyn had seen the entry code when she had clicked on the *Quarantine* section on the computer screen. She recited the long number to herself as she walked along: 30041954.

Why would any area in the house need such an elaborate security system? *Because there's something secret in there*, thought Tamsyn. *That's why.*

The door had a small glass panel in it – like a porthole. Tamsyn peered through the glass. The sharp intake of her breath echoed along the enclosed corridor.

She had expected to see a fairly ordinary room. What she actually saw was something quite different and totally astonishing.

She tapped out the security code and the lock released with a metallic click. She pushed the door wide and stepped through it into some kind of weird sci-fi dream world.

The annexe didn't consist of a single room, but a whole series of rooms, leading into each other. Large rooms with white walls. And now the reason for the lack of windows became clear. The whole of the roof was constructed of glass panels. Over some of the panels, blinds had been drawn, but enough were open to the sky for Tamsyn to see perfectly clearly the nature of the place she had stumbled upon.

There were no doorways, just wide arches linking one room to another. The walls of each room were lined with cages and tanks and pens. And in nearly every one was an animal. There was an entire miniature zoo in here!

Tamsyn dragged a box over to prevent the door from closing itself behind her. Then she walked through the rooms in a kind of daze. There were reptiles and lizards; there were small furry mammals that scuttled and dug. Occasionally, she saw a creature she vaguely recognized – but most were of species completely unknown to her. There was cage after cage of brightly coloured birds. Some began screeching when they caught sight of her – a sad, terrible sound in that sterile place.

Then she saw it! Crouched miserably in the back of one cage: the golden lion tamarin. She made comforting cooing sounds as she pressed her nose against the thin bars of the animal's new prison. She stretched her fingers out through the grille to try and show that she was a friend. The tamarin stared hollowly at her and shivered.

If her guess was right, then this whole place was full of illegally imported animals. An illegal secret zoo where Don Van Meer could come and gloat over his helpless captives! Tamsyn shuddered at the thought.

She had to get out of there and get help!

She saw a small desk with a computer terminal standing on it. The screen was smaller than she was used to. It was filled with a static display of numbered and coded boxes.

Tamsyn reached for the mouse. If the computer was linked to the outside world through a modem, then she'd be able to use it to get help.

'You can't keep me here,' Rob said, staring up into Van Meer's icy eyes. 'We know what you've been doing.'

Van Meer leaned over Rob's chair. He was obviously very angry.

'We know about the tamarin,' Rob said levelly. 'And we're going to tell the police.' He attempted what he hoped looked like a triumphant smile. 'In fact, my friend is probably on to them right this minute!'

Van Meer gave a snarl of rage and twisted away, as if he needed a few seconds to gather his thoughts. He stiffened, staring at something on the far side of his office.

Rob followed the line of his eyes. It was a plain white door. The door was slightly ajar.

Van Meer turned on Rob again with a ferocious glint in his eyes.

'Maybe not!' he muttered as he rounded Rob's chair and pushed him towards the door. 'Maybe not!'

Van Meer hauled the door open and Rob found himself staring along a white-walled corridor.

'I think we'd better go and see what your friend is up to,' Van Meer said as he pushed Rob inside. 'She might need our help. There are some dangerous animals in there. We wouldn't want anyone to be accidentally bitten by a taipan.' Van Meer's voice lowered ominously. 'Not accidentally.'

'What does that mean?' Rob asked.

'Don't you know what a taipan is, boy? It's a venomous snake. I have a few of the *rarer* kind here. Very dangerous. I've got blacksnakes and death adders and puff adders and king cobras. I've got boa constrictors and pythons, too. Oh, I've got a *lot* of animals in here that you wouldn't want to meet on a dark night.' Van Meer leaned close over Rob's head and whispered in his ear. 'Scorpions, venomous spiders, poisonous toads, vipers,' he chuckled. 'You name it, I've got it. All *exclusive* varieties, of course. I even have a few special fish. Some have the most amazingly vicious, poison-tipped spines. A person could die within four days.' He clicked his tongue. 'Isn't nature amazing? The number of different ways in which a poor, unsuspecting person can come a real cropper is quite astounding – quite astounding! And all of them here. In my world. For my *personal* viewing.'

Van Meer was beginning to sound completely demented.

It had only taken Tamsyn a few seconds to discover that the computer wasn't linked to anything outside the complex of cellar rooms.

She realized that this was a simple workhorse computer. It had been a little over-optimistic of her to think otherwise. After all, not every computer in the world was on the Internet.

This machine was a central control system designed to keep the various cages and tanks at particular temperatures, and to switch lights on and off, and, in many cases, so it seemed, to automatically provide the animals with the required food and drink.

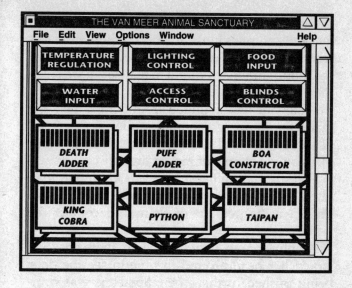

File   Edit   View   Options   Window   Help

TEMPERATURE REGULATION   LIGHTING CONTROL   FOOD INPUT

WATER INPUT   ACCESS CONTROL   BLINDS CONTROL

DEATH ADDER   PUFF ADDER   BOA CONSTRICTOR

KING COBRA   PYTHON   TAIPAN

It made sense, Tamsyn thought. This horrible place was obviously a secret – Van Meer could hardly be popping in here every few minutes to check that his captives were OK.

She clicked on *Access Control* and a different screen dropped down. It was clear that Access Control was a computerized method of opening and closing the tanks and cages. At the bottom of the menu was a panel:

ACCESS WHICH HOLDING AREA?

She typed in: ALL. A panel appeared.

EXECUTE? YES / NO

Tamsyn hesitated. Her gut reaction had been to let all the animals loose; to liberate them from this terrible prison. But it only took a couple of seconds of rational thought to realize what a crazy idea that was.

A sibilant hiss sounded from behind her. She glanced around. A seemingly endless knotted coil of some huge snake moved slowly behind thick glass only a couple of metres away.

No, she couldn't just let them loose like that. She decided that the best thing she could do for them was to get out of there and contact the police.

A split second later she heard footsteps. She jerked her head around in time to see the door being pushed further open. Someone was coming. She didn't hesitate. Tamsyn dived for cover behind one of the partitions and held her breath as she listened for what would come next.

She heard more footsteps then a man's voice.

'There's no point in hiding, girl! Come on out. Nothing's going to happen to you.'

Tamsyn listened to the deafening hammering of her heart as she pressed herself against the far side of the partition. What on earth was she to do? There were no windows and no other doors. She was trapped.

'We can sort this out, girl,' Van Meer called. 'There's no need to be silly. Show yourself or I'll have to make things uncomfortable for your friend here!'

He had Rob with him!

'See?' She heard Rob's voice. 'She's not in here.'

'I'll count to three,' Van Meer called, ignoring Rob. 'One. Two.'

Tamsyn stepped out of hiding. A sinister smile slid across Van Meer's face. He was standing beside Rob. They were right next to the computer desk.

'That's better,' he said. 'Now then, what are we going to do with you two?'

Suddenly Rob lunged with his arm, spinning his chair so that it struck Van Meer, and then hit out again while the man was off-balance.

'Run, Tamsyn!' Rob yelled.

She bolted for the door. It was shut. Van Meer had kicked aside the box that she had used to prevent the automatic locking-device from activating – cutting off her escape.

She only had a couple of seconds to act. She hammered the code into the silver box. *30441954.*

Nothing happened. Tamsyn let out a gasp of anger and despair. She'd entered the wrong code. For once in her life, her remarkable memory had failed her – and at such a dreadful time!

Van Meer staggered. He grabbed hold of Rob's collar and wrenched Rob almost out of his chair. Rob flailed around as Van Meer's arm locked around his neck and tightened. The room began to spin, but as the computer screen whirled in front of Rob's swimming eyes, he saw the YES/NO panel. He had no idea what command he was activating as he wrenched forwards and brought his hand down on the Y key. He hoped desperately that whatever happened, it would be something which would distract Van Meer from strangling him.

A moment later the cellar was filled with a series of clicks and whirrs as every cage and tank began to open.

Van Meer released Rob and threw himself towards Tamsyn. He crashed against the door as she ducked out of his way. She made the only move open to her: she turned and ran deeper into the long annexe. With a low growl, Van Meer leaped after her.

Rob stared around himself in a panic. Everywhere it seemed, glass panels were sliding open. Lids were hydraulically rising. Cage doors were standing wide apart. Through the archways he could see that some of the more inquisitive animals were already coming out of their cages. And a couple of metres away from him, the long, thick coils of a large snake were unrolling themselves as a narrow, wedge-shaped head slid over the threshold of the tank.

CHAPTER 13

Tamsyn bolted into the room where the monkeys were kept. All the doors were wide open and the air was filled with a cacophony of noises as the animals began to take advantage of their sudden freedom. It seemed that the whole room was filled with small hairy shapes, scampering across the floor, swinging from cage to cage, chattering and screeching.

Tamsyn almost tripped over one small creature as it scuttled across the floor. Van Meer was nearly on her. Then she really did trip, falling heavily against iron bars. She just had time to see Van Meer's shadow looming over her before there was a flurry of movement and a wild screeching.

Tamsyn twisted onto her back. A familiar, maddened ball of golden fur seemed to be attached to Van Meer's face. He prized it off with both hands and hurled the screaming tamarin across the room.

'You monster!' Tamsyn yelled. She threw her full weight at Van Meer's legs. He tottered and fell forwards into one of the larger cages. Tamsyn saw him strike his head on the top of the entrance as he fell.

'Rob!' she yelled. 'Shut the cages! Now!'

Tamsyn staggered to her feet, casting around for some weapon with which she could defend herself. Out of the corner of her eye she could see birds flitting through the air.

Van Meer was lying face down in the straw. He didn't move. The blow must have stunned him.

'Got it!' she heard Rob yell. 'There you go!'

The cage doors began to swing closed. All around her she could hear the click and snick of locks. But in many cases the animals that would have been behind those doors were already roaming free.

Tamsyn felt something grip her leg. She looked down. It was the tamarin. It seemed none the worse for its ordeal. Very cautiously, so as not to alarm it, Tamsyn crouched and gathered the animal up in her arms.

Long, thin arms wrapped around her neck. She walked slowly and carefully back into the room where Rob was sitting.

'Van Meer's knocked himself out,' she gasped. 'He's in one of the cages. Serves him right, too! We ought to just leave him there! Rob, what's wrong?'

Rob's eyes were as round as saucers and he had a panicky look on his face that she'd never seen before.

And then Tamsyn saw the problem. A vast snake was slowly gliding across the floor towards Rob.

'I think it's a boa,' Tamsyn said, her mouth suddenly dry. 'Don't make any sudden moves, Rob.' The snake had to be at least four metres long.

'OK,' whispered Rob. 'I'm not making any sudden moves. Can you get past me to the door and get us out of here?'

'There's a problem with that,' Tamsyn said. 'I can't remember the code.'

Rob almost jumped clear of his chair. 'What?'

'Calm down,' Tamsyn said. 'You'll frighten the snake. And don't move.'

The wicked-looking head of the snake was perilously close to Rob now.

'I'll frighten *it*?' Rob groaned. 'I like that!'

'I'll think of something,' Tamsyn said.

In the following silence the snake lifted its head and seemed to be sniffing or checking out Rob's shoes. Rob went almost rigid with fear. A long tongue flickered as the head lifted and the coils gathered themselves.

'Um, I don't want to be a nuisance,' Rob croaked. 'But if you've got a plan, now would be a good time to put it into action.' He tried to look at her without moving his head.

The snake reared to the level of Rob's knees.

'No problem,' Tamsyn croaked. 'I'll just get around behind it and drag it away from you.'

'Are you sure about that?' Rob said from between gritted teeth.

'Er … yes,' Tamsyn stepped sideways, eyeing the thick far end of the snake uneasily. She'd heard of taking a tiger by the tail – but a snake? The tamarin clung closer to her as she crept forwards with tiny steps.

She was startled by a small, scuttling green shape that shot out from a corner of the room. It scooted across the floor in a flurry of scampering legs and dived under the desk. It was some sort of lizard that Tamsyn's movements had disturbed.

The snake's head turned in an instant and Rob let out a gasp of relief as the front end of the snake lunged under the desk.

Rob slammed his hands down on the wheel-rims of his chair and sped backwards, away from the huge snake.

Tamsyn ran forward towards the main door. The tamarin gripped ever more tightly on to her, its sharp little claws digging into the flesh of her neck.

30441945.

The door remained stubbornly closed.

'Tamsyn! Watch out!'

She glanced around and saw a thin black snake slithering towards her. The tamarin made a nervous whimpering noise.

'It's OK,' she whispered as she backed away from the door. 'I'll get us out of here. Somehow.'

'Have you remembered the code?' Rob asked.

'Not exactly.'

'This isn't looking good,' Rob said, staring down at the black snake. 'You know all about animals, Tamsyn. What should we do?'

Suddenly Tamsyn gave a shriek which nearly scared the life out of Rob. 'Josh!'

Rob looked round. Never in his life had he been more glad to see his friend's face than at that moment when it peered so unexpectedly through the glass porthole of the locked annexe door.

Josh flapped a hand for an instant and then the door swung open.

'What on earth are you two—'

'Josh! Watch out!' Tamsyn shouted.

Josh followed the line of her eyes. The black snake was rising to strike.

But Josh didn't give it the chance. He threw his backpack at the black shape and together they went skidding across the floor.

'Let's get out of here!' Tamsyn yelled, holding on to the tamarin as she dived for the door, only a split second behind Rob.

Josh slammed the door behind them.

'I called the police,' he said. 'They should be here in a couple of minutes.'

'How did you know where we were?' Rob gasped.

Josh grinned. 'Elementary, my dear Rob. Elementary!'

*

The police arrived about five minutes
later. Van Meer was awake by then. You
should have seen his face as they
marched him off! Anyway, the police let
us stay until the RSPCA got there to try
and sort the mess out. According to one
of the RSPCA people, virtually all the
animals down there were endangered
species. Van Meer had been collecting
them illegally for years.
Lauren and Mitch, although you both
really helped a lot, it was Tom who
finally saved the day! Cheers, Tom! If
Josh hadn't read your message about
Donald Van Meer, he wouldn't have
rushed there in the nick of time to save
us from being swallowed whole by a
very large snake.

'You're not kidding,' said Rob, reading over
Tamsyn's shoulder. 'That thing was up for eating
me, chair and all! Tell them about what the police
found on Van Meer's computer.'

'I was just going to,' Tamsyn said. 'It's difficult
to concentrate with you hanging over one shoulder and Josh hanging over the other!'

The police took a look at Van Meer's
computer and found whole files full of
information about all his dodgy imports
over the past few years.

The police reckon they'll be able to
track down all Van Meer's contacts and
prosecutions are bound to follow.
Including for the man who brought the
tamarin over here and a couple of crew
members of the Stonewall Jay who were in
on the deal.
And it serves them right!

'What about your tamarin?' Josh said. 'Tell
them about that.'

'Who's writing this?'

'You are.'

'Right!'

Temporary homes have been found for
a few of the animals from Van Meer's
private zoo, but the RSPCA are very
worried about what's going happen to
most of them, which is really sad. But
it's not all doom and gloom. A temporary
place has been found for my tamarin, so
at least he'll be looked after until he
can be shipped back home again where he
belongs!

'Ahem!' Rob said. 'Tell them what name the
tamarin has been given.'

Tamsyn's face was split by a broad grin as she
continued to type.

By the way, the golden lion tamarin who
started the whole thing off is being
looked after at a veterinary college
only a few miles away, so I'll be able
to go and visit him a few times before
he gets sent back to Brazil. Oh, and the
RSPCA have given it a name. Tamsyn the
tamarin!
Thanks for everything you did, people!
We couldn't have managed without you!
Best wishes,
Tamsyn – not the tamarin, the *human*!

Mail:

michael coleman

WEB TRAP

A click of the mouse and it was done.
'Stealing is so easy,' Tamsyn said.

How can new videos, music and computer games be offered for sale on the Net before they've even been released? And how does a famous TV star fit into the picture?
Rob needs answers fast: the future of his parents' company depends on it. With Tamsyn, Josh and his friends on the Net he gathers pieces of evidence from all corners of the globe until just one is missing. And the only way to find that is to set a trap – a trap that could go horribly wrong . . .

Other books in the series ▷

michael coleman

ESCAPE KEY

The man's face stared out at them from the computer screen.
'It is him!' exclaimed Rob.

The photograph, flashed instantly from Australia via the Internet, sets Rob, Tamsyn and Josh on a thrilling hunt for a man wanted by the police on two continents. They've seen him once already, but they've no idea where he is now. With the help of brilliant detective work by their friends on the Net, they start to track down their mysterious suspect . . .

Other books in the series ▷